For Martin

Katharine McMahon is the author of seven novels, including the Richard & Judy Book Club selected *The Rose of Sebastopol*. She lives with her family in Hertfordshire. Visit her website at www.katharinemcmahon.com

By Katharine McMahon

The Crimson Rooms
The Rose of Sebastopol
The Alchemist's Daughter
A Way Through the Woods
Footsteps
Confinement
After Mary

A Way Through The Woods

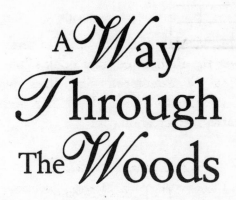

KATHARINE MCMAHON

PHOENIX

PHOENIX PAPERBACK

First published in Great Britain in 1990
by Sinclair-Stevenson Limited
This paperback edition published in 2009
by Phoenix,
an imprint of Orion Books Ltd,
Orion House, 5 Upper St Martin's Lane,
London WC2H 9EA

An Hachette UK company

3 5 7 9 10 8 6 4 2

A CIP catalogue record for this book
is available from the British Library.

ISBN 978 0 7538 2546 4

Typeset at The Spartan Press Ltd,
Lymington, Hants

Printed in Great Britain by Clays Ltd, St Ives plc

The Orion Publishing Group's policy is to use papers
that are natural, renewable and recyclable products and
made from wood grown in sustainable forests. The logging
and manufacturing processes are expected to conform to
the environmental regulations of the country of origin.

www.orionbooks.co.uk

They shut the road through the woods
Seventy years ago.
Weather and rain have undone it again,
And now you would never know
There was once a road through the woods
Before they planted the trees.

It is underneath the coppice and heath,
And the thin anemones.
Only the keeper sees
That, where the ring-dove broods,
And the badgers roll at ease,
There was once a way through the woods.

Yet, if you enter the woods
Of a summer evening late,
When the night air cools on the trout-ringed pools
Where the otter whistles his mate,
(They fear not men in the woods,
Because they see so few)
You will hear the beat of a horse's feet,
And the swish of a skirt in the dew,
Steadily cantering through
The misty solitudes,
As though they perfectly knew
The old lost road through the woods . . .
But there is no road through the woods!

The Way Through the Woods
RUDYARD KIPLING

I

May 1920

John Gresham was shown into a joyless drawing-room.
No fire burned in the grate, not a speck of dust softened
the polished bureau or chair legs, even the late spring
flowers stood meekly to attention in symmetrical arrays
of pink and white. A blend of gold, cream and subdued
green, the room gave no indication that the mistress of
the house was a young woman, unless perhaps by the
translucent gleam of over-elaborate lace curtains. Near
the plain mantel was a small inlaid table, its purpose to
support two photographs. One must be of Nicholas; the
face beneath the uniform cap displayed clear-cut features
in half profile. The second, oblong mounted, was presumably Sophia, though John Gresham scarcely recognised her thin face under hair swept back in pre-war
fashion, her remote gaze and mouth softened only by
vaseline on the kind camera lens.

Hearing footsteps, he replaced the portrait, turned to
the door and there she was, rather less delicate-featured
than in the photograph, very pale, her puzzled eyes
revealing the correct degree of welcome.

'Mr Gresham. What a pleasant surprise.'

'I'm sorry to have disturbed you. I wanted to come in person.'

She offered him tea but no, he would not stay, he had an appointment later.

'First, let me congratulate you on your engagement,' he said. 'I read the announcement and of course your Aunt Margaret was very full of it.'

She smiled self-consciously and clasped her hands as if to hide the ring.

'But I'm afraid it's as the executor of my wife's will that I've come. Eleanor died, you know, in March.'

Her poise fractured, she looked genuinely upset. 'Mrs Gresham! I had no idea. Oh I'm so sorry.'

'Yes, well, she had been very ill for a long time, as you were perhaps aware.'

'No, I hadn't realised. I'm sorry. I'm rather out of touch with my aunt and people in Needlewick.'

'The fact is my wife left you something and I thought . . . as it might seem . . . Well, I had other business in town so I thought I'd come.'

She was watching him now with some warmth. 'Really I hardly knew her. I can't think why she should leave me anything.'

'Oh, it's very small, terribly small, just a couple of notebooks – they were Helen's. I know, it's very odd, but my wife particularly wanted you to have them. She only made the will in February, you see, and was still very much in her right mind. I couldn't refuse her.'

'But how extraordinary! What about Helen? Doesn't she want them?'

'No, no. I wrote to her and checked. She replied that

Eleanor had discussed it with her. Really she would rather the notebooks were thrown away, she said, but she thought it was up to Eleanor as she'd had them for years. Helen gave them to her a long time ago. Helen didn't want them, and apparently Eleanor asked for them.'

Sophia's posture had altered, so that she leaned forward in her chair, her hands clenched together. 'It was very kind of you to have come all this way to bring them to me.'

'No, I was in town. But I haven't got the notebooks with me. That was the other thing – Eleanor stipulated that you have to collect them in person. They're in Needlewick. It's silly, I know. I would understand if you didn't bother. I'll put them away or burn them if you'd rather.'

Sophia now collapsed back, laughing. 'Really, it's most peculiar. What a mystery. Well, Mr Gresham, I'm afraid I can't say that I've any plans to come to Needlewick at the moment. Colin and I intend to marry in September, you see. Quite soon. There's lots to be done.'

'Of course.' He drew his feet together, ready for departure. They both stood.

'I'll let you know what I decide, shall I?' she asked, leading him into the hall and opening the front door for him.

'Yes, yes, there's no hurry.'

She shook his hand. 'It really was very kind of you to come.'

'Not at all, not at all.'

Sophia watched Mr Gresham walk hurriedly away, a slight figure, much too frail. She had scarcely known

3

him before except as a self-effacing, masculine presence yet his smile now seemed welcome and familiar to her. Poor Mr Gresham, all alone.

She closed the heavy door and stood for a moment smoothing her dress and hair. The visit had left her in a state of nervous excitement. Mrs Gresham was dead.

Upstairs, Sophia stood at a mirror, arrested by the sight of her reflection with its unusually flushed cheeks. She remembered Eleanor Gresham in her garden, the lawn ripe at her feet, a breeze stirring the brim of her hat and the ruffles of her gown.

Sophia turned abruptly from the glass and, though it was far too early, began to dress for dinner. Colin was expected and it was worth taking considerable trouble for him because he always noticed what she wore – his delight in every aspect of herself was perhaps what she most liked about him. It was a pity that, as the hours ticked by, she tended to be oppressed by the combined company of Colin and her father. Neither could be natural with the other; it annoyed her particularly that her father's behaviour should be so deferential. She would have to insist on going out for a walk with Colin after dinner, although that would mean kisses; hand kisses, cheek kisses she liked, mouth kisses seemed intrusive and a little dirty. It was as if they were being performed under the approving eye of her father even when he was far away.

Carefully reknotting her hair, she speculated on the contents of Mrs Gresham's will. 'The woman didn't even like me,' she would later tell Colin – she mentally rehearsed the words. 'She thought I was bad for Helen, I could tell. Oh, haven't I told you about my cousin, Helen Callwood? I went to stay with her in 1909 when I was just fourteen because Nicholas had measles. It was thought I'd be safer away from the germs so they sent me to my mother's sister, Aunt Margaret, and her husband, a doctor, and my cousin Helen, in a remote village called Needlewick.'

That was such a strange summer, she thought. Very odd indeed. And then she hurried away to check the flowers on the dinner table because she didn't want to think about Needlewick any more.

No meal in the presence of Simon Theobald could be comfortable; even Sophia who had dined alone with her father for a number of years was never at ease and poor Colin compensated for his anxiety by over-zealous attempts at conversation, clashing of cutlery and conscientious lip-wiping.

There were elements in Simon Theobald's domestic life which he had failed to control so, as if in compensation, he now insisted ever more rigidly on the rituals learnt in childhood. Food must be perfectly served, neither he nor Sophia was permitted to speak without first laying down knife and fork and resting hands on lap, no drop of wine or gravy must splash on the white cloth. At the end of each course Theobald would cleanse imaginary crumbs from his fingertips by flicking his thumbs across them several times. Sophia was aware of her father's every indrawn breath and click of teeth. The sight of a soft pudding made her jaw muscles clench in anticipation of the unnecessary grinding of his molars through unresisting blancmange. For her, company at dinner was a blissful distraction. Colin's proposal, so acceptable to her father, had also released her from the torture of meal times; she ceased to be the unwilling focus of all her father's attention and might even laugh or blow her nose.

'Mr Gresham called today, Father.'

His mouth was full of lamb and young peas. In the time it took him to prepare for speech she had begun to regret this rash revelation.

'Mr Gresham?' His clear blue gaze, from eyes remarkably large and lavishly lashed, met hers in polite interest.

'Do you not remember the name? He's a lawyer in Needlewick. I met him when I went to stay there years ago, when Nicholas was ill. Eleanor, his wife, was a great friend of mother's.'

'I know who Mr Gresham is.'

'Where's Needlewick?' Colin asked.

Now that she had opened the Pandora's Box, Sophia would have given a great deal to close it again. Already her father's neat movements with knife and fork had become yet more deliberate.

'It's the tiny village where my mother was born,' she told Colin.

'Ah.' Colin shot a hurried glance at his host and reached for the dish of potatoes – a spoon bounced on the cloth and flicked spots of melted butter on to the salt cellar.

'Yes, I spent a summer there once with my aunt and uncle. The Greshams were family friends also living in the village. It seems that Mrs Gresham has left some books for me in her will. She died. Did you know that, father?'

'I believe it might have been mentioned in your uncle's last letter to me.'

'But how exciting,' said Colin, 'are they of any value, these books?'

'I shouldn't think so. Why didn't you tell me Mrs Gresham was dead, Father?'

There was another long pause while Theobald finished his meal and pushed the plate a fraction of an inch away. 'I had no idea you would be interested. You've never mentioned her.'

'She was Mother's dearest friend.'

'I don't remember your mother ever writing to her much.'

Colin came crashing to the rescue. 'Talking of writing – I've been defending a fearfully interesting case today. Fraud. Incredible the lengths people will go to . . .'

They walked along the Embankment, the wind tossing litter and flying blossom about their ankles so that Sophia shivered.

'It's so cold for May.'

Colin drew her closer by tucking her arm through his. 'You're not wearing enough. You never do.'

'I wanted to get out quickly. Good God, Colin, I don't know how you can bear the atmosphere in that house. You must be mad to inflict it on yourself.'

'I'd do far worse for you, Sophia.'

'I know you would. I know.'

'I sometimes wonder why you deliberately provoke him by talking about your mother.'

'I don't do it to provoke him – not entirely. Colin, she's my mother! I have to keep her alive for myself, I do precious little else for her.'

'Has she written lately?'

When they talked about her mother, she always felt that Colin's compassionate tone would be more suitable if he were discussing someone dangerously ill or dead. 'You know she doesn't write. Why should she, I never write to her.' Her raised voice attracted the interest of other strollers. 'I think my mother will be very sad to know Eleanor Gresham is dead. I wish I'd known her better. I can't think why she thought of me when she was writing her will.'

Overhead cherry blossom hung in dim clusters. Mrs Gresham; the cow parsley in the bank outside her house, her garden hazed by yellow heat and the roses full-blown.

At breakfast two days later the letter arrived confirming Sophie's unusual legacy. She pushed the envelope to one side and spread butter on her toast.

'You received the letter from Gresham, then?'

'Yes.' She shielded her face from sunlight spilling through the long voile curtains. 'It's absurd. I can't go all the way to Needlewick for such a silly thing. I've far too much to do.'

'Although, as I've said, Sophia, you ought to visit your uncle and aunt before your marriage. You could collect your book then.' Simon Theobald had in part made his fortune by never turning down a gift or an opportunity.

'Maybe, yes.'

But later, after her father had left the house, Sophia raged about the rooms. What did Helen's diary contain that could be of relevance now? Why had it been given to Eleanor Gresham? And why should Sophia go to Needlewick when Mr Gresham might so easily have posted it or indeed delivered it himself? Perhaps Mrs Gresham had grown eccentric in the late stages of her illness.

But curiosity burned; Sophia knew she must read the diary which would of course contain many references to her own visit in that summer of 1909. And Needlewick was not so very far away; she need only stay overnight or Colin could even motor her up in a day. But she did not want Colin in Needlewick. The thought brought her up short before a large oval mirror on the landing as if she'd suddenly been caught rehearsing the name of a secret lover.

Finally, for reassurance, she opened the door of her brother's room and recoiled, as always, from the fact of his complete absence. The shutters were closed and in the grey light from the doorway the room was dim and very tidy.

Closing the door, she went to the bed and laid her head on the pillow. Nicholas, I wrote to you so often in the Needlewick summer. Do you remember how home-sick I was — how you-sick? I would have caught your measles willingly rather than be exiled like that.

She stood up and whispered fiercely: 'I'll go, I'll go.'

It would be her last trip without Colin for some time — she'd tell him that for sentimental reasons she must make it alone. Anyway, he wouldn't be interested in girlish memories.

'I'll go then, shall I, Nicholas?'

Her words fell on the soft carpet, the empty bookshelves and the smooth quilt, where they died softly with no ears to hear them.

2

Mrs Deborah Parditer, now widowed, had become a frequent visitor to Middlecote Hall, Needlewick. She enjoyed the drive, the change of scenery and the fact that from her vantage point of the Hall she could venture forth to sample at first hand all the goings-on of a village whose inhabitants were as familiar to her as when she lived there as a child. Besides, Deborah felt that it was her duty to go often. She was needed at the Hall. Her sister, Lady Jane Middlecote, would be dreary without Deborah's energetic pursuit of diversion.

During this year's Whitsun visit, it became apparent that there was much of interest afoot. The sisters ordered tea in the drawing-room, safe in the knowledge that Sir George was absent for the day and they might therefore enjoy hours of uninterrupted conversation. Deborah established herself in the bay window, thereby gaining a lookout over the valley and, to the east, the village.

'And how is poor George?' she asked.

'Still too heavy, I'm afraid. I do worry. He gets terribly puffy-looking, even after just a little exercise or a glass of port.'

'But he won't be moderate, I suppose? Gerald was the same.' There was a sombre pause for Gerald Parditer's memory to be decently celebrated between the sisters, during which Deborah's eye fell on the chair-backs. 'You decided on the new antimacassars, then? I think white is the right choice – cream would soon have seemed tired.'

'I leave George's old one tucked down the side of his chair for the evenings.'

Deborah's attention had strayed to the garden which looked just as it should for May; its borders, arbours and paths pleasing to the eye but unremarkable. Every aspect of Jane's life had that same air of neatness and quality – only imagination lacked.

'The river looks very full.'

'We've had so much rain. It flooded earlier in the month – nearly covered the bridge.'

Deborah's gaze had now fallen on distant Round-stones, squat behind its white wall. 'And how is Margaret?'

Lady Middlecote crossed to her work-table and took out her knitting, fine wool on slender needles. 'Look what I'm making for the bazaar, Deborah, a shawl.'

'You'll ruin your eyes with such close work. They'll only sell it for a shilling or two, you'll see. You might just as well have knitted something thick and serviceable.'

The lace shawl hung like a cobweb against Jane's fingers. 'Some girl will appreciate it, I'm sure.' Jane settled herself near the window. 'You were asking about the Callwoods. Harry is much as ever. They're both well. But Margaret is in a state because Sophia Theobald is coming to stay on Saturday for several days.'

'*Sophia!* Really?'

Lady Middlecote ran her finger along the close print of the pattern, twined the yarn once round her third finger, twice round the middle, over the index, knitted a stitch, wound the wool three times round the needle.

'She's coming to collect the diary, then? John Gresham wrote to her, I suppose,' Deborah prompted at last, exasperated by the delay. Jane was deliberately making her wait for information.

'Of course. He had to, as he was the executor. But Margaret says Sophia is coming mainly because she is so soon to be married and wishes to visit her relations first.'

'Nonsense, the girl has no family feeling whatever,' said Deborah.

'How long is it since she was here?' asked Jane, having completed another stitch.

'I can tell you exactly. She came to my Catherine's wedding in August 1909. What a day! Do you remember the thunderstorm? Of course, we invited all the Callwoods and as Sophia was staying they brought her. Poor Helen, I did feel sorry for her.'

'Why?'

'I'm sure Sophia was too much for her. I don't think Helen ever recovered from that visit, she was never satisfied after that.'

'But she's had an extraordinary life,' said Jane. 'She's certainly got what she wanted.'

'You think so? I wonder.' Deborah's eye was still on Roundstones. 'So Sophia is coming to Needlewick! She won't find it much changed, will she? A few male faces gone. No Helen to bully.'

'She didn't bully Helen.'

'Of course she did. Helen was asking to be bullied. Don't you remember? I remember her to this day at the wedding breakfast; eyes fixed on Sophia's face, always seeking approval. She worshipped her! It must have driven Sophia mad. In the end, though, I suppose it did Helen good, made her grow up a bit, put an end to her tramping about the countryside.'

There was a tense pause broken hurriedly by Jane. 'I'm afraid Margaret will wear herself out getting the house ready. She's starting on the spare room this morning.'

'How inconsiderate of Sophia to have given so little notice! She should have realised Margaret would find it hard to cope.'

'How could she know? They can't have met since the brother's funeral in the war and I remember Margaret telling me afterwards that Sophia was so distraught she could hardly speak to anyone. She was very fond of her brother.'

'We'll call on Margaret this afternoon,' Deborah Parditer announced decisively, 'and try to calm her down.'

Roundstones was a white, asymmetrical house set apart from Needlewick. The lane which ran westwards along the valley climbed steeply away from the village parallel to the River Needle and passed only feet from the front door. The house, lying high and isolated on the side of the valley, commanded sweeping views across to Middlecote Hall and Needlewick and in the other direction the river could be traced for some considerable distance. The garden fell steeply away, neatly bordered by a high stone wall as if to keep house and grounds from tumbling headlong into the river. At the lower end of the wall, beyond the smooth lawn and wide flowerbeds was a little green door giving access to the river path and the foot-bridge. Roundstones had been the home of Needlewick doctors for several generations and when the previous incumbent died the house had passed to his eldest daughter, Margaret and her new husband, Dr Harry Callwood.

The housekeeper, Mrs Bubb – nobody knew her first name – answered the door to Lady Middlecote and her sister. 'She's in the drawing-room,' she said and shuffled off to the kitchen stairs.

The sisters walked through the hall to the back room where Margaret Callwood was at the mantelpiece dusting her collection of china cats. She turned guiltily to face her visitors as if caught in some underhand activity. 'I thought I'd just run a cloth over as Sophia's coming – did Jane tell you? But how are you, Deborah? You do look well. What a wonderful hat, I'm sure I haven't seen it before. How was the drive? Is Mrs Bubb making tea, do you think? Perhaps I should help her, we've been very busy. The spare room needed quite a going over, it's been unused for so long.'

Deborah Parditer gave her hat a gratified pat and seated herself in an armchair near the window. 'I would sit down if I were you, Margaret. You look as if you could do with a rest. I'm quite sure Mrs Bubb is capable of bringing the tea. You don't want to upset her.'

But Margaret still wavered at the door.

'The garden is looking wonderful, Margaret,' said kind Jane Middlecote. 'I was telling Deborah that your garden here at Roundstones is particularly splendid this year.'

The lure was irresistible; Margaret moved at once to

the window. 'The April rain helped. I'm particularly pleased with the azaleas.'

'The garden is a delight! Sophia has chosen just the right time to visit. I hope you're not going to overdo it, Margaret, you look a little pale. She's only your niece.'

'I am rather alarmed. Oh, Mrs Bubb, how kind. Do let me!' Margaret darted from her chair to hold the door back. Tea was laid efficiently, though gracelessly, by Mrs Bubb who picked up the discarded china cloth before closing the door behind her. 'Oh dear. She cleaned in here this morning but she's never liked the cats so she doesn't bother with them much. And Sophia was rather grand even when she was only thirteen and now she's marrying into the peerage – and anyway, I feel bound to put myself out for my poor sister's daughter.'

'I suppose you've heard nothing from Suzanna?' Deborah asked. Removing the teapot lid from her hostess's preoccupied grasp, she stirred the leaves and poured the tea.

'Not a word, not since Christmas when she sent that little Swiss postcard.'

'I remember. And as usual, the card told us precisely nothing. But Suzanna's hand-writing bothered me,' said Margaret. 'It seemed so unlike her usual, though perhaps it was written in a hurry. Oh thank you, Deborah. Yes, three lumps. And do have a scone – I don't know how Mrs Bubb found the time. You see she doesn't like Sophia and that makes it worse.'

'But the girl hasn't been here for years. How can Mrs Bubb not like her?'

'I think she found her very trying that summer, you

know. There was always a bit of an atmosphere because Sophia wasn't used to helping out with meals or with her bed, and Mrs Bubb isn't one to forget. And she misses Helen so much, I think she somehow begrudges Sophia's visit because she'd rather it were Helen.'

'I understand John told Sophia about the will?'

'Oh yes, but I'm sure she's not coming for that. Good Lord, I hope she doesn't bother with that old diary of Helen's, I can't imagine it could have any interest for her. I really cannot understand Eleanor, it's such an extraordinary thing to have done.'

'For John Gresham's sake,' murmured Jane, 'I'm glad Sophia is coming to collect the wretched diary. It'll be all finished with then.'

'I wish she wouldn't,' Margaret suddenly exclaimed. 'I wish Sophie wouldn't read it.'

3

Sophia travelled to Needlewick by train, this time alone. She sat by the window in a first class compartment and watched her elusive reflection in the window as she remembered her previous trip to Needlewick in the summer of 1909, when she was just fourteen. Perched opposite, then, had been Miss Pinner, governess, whom Sophia had always insisted should be called a *companion*. Sophia could still recall the irritation of being in Miss Pinner's company, the violent distaste she had felt for the woman's sad brown hair, yellow front teeth and mouth that never closed. I must have been a terrible charge, she reflected, nerves screaming when she touched me, every ounce of ingenuity directed at making her life as unpleasant as possible. I don't suppose I spoke once all the way on the train or even said goodbye at Cheltenham. I believe I may even have tipped her! The memory of this insult caused Sophia to shift in the seat and turn away from the window. And the luggage I insisted on bringing with me – all those dresses and no one at home with the energy to dissuade me. They just let me bring it all. Still, Helen appreciated it. And Sophia thought of how Helen's long hair had dangled over the side of the trunk as she peered at her cousin's London finery.

Sophia was tired. Preparations for this visit had been

exhausting because she had felt considerable reluctance, a desire to hold back. And her father had been irritable all week. 'After all,' she told Colin. 'I can understand why he doesn't really like the thought of me in Needlewick. The place has painful associations because it's where he and mother met. But on the other hand, he always likes to do what's right, and in his book girls should pay pre-wedding visits to their relations. It's my heritage after all, and I'm not so well-endowed with relatives that I can afford to lose touch with any.'

Because she was excluding Colin from Needlewick she had treated him with unusual kindness during the week prior to her departure, grateful that he didn't question her excuses. 'My aunt is a worrier, you see. It would kill her to have to entertain a real peer. She'd think she ought to slaughter a swan from the Needle at the very least.'

'She'll have to meet me some day.'

'Yes, at our wedding, but that won't be nearly such an ordeal for her, there'll be so many people.'

So now she was travelling to Needlewick alone, the weight of being someone's daughter, someone's fiancée temporarily left behind. The train steamed through frothy May embankments, woods floating on the purple haze of bluebells, eager green fields. Wonderful train taking me away, taking me away, taking me away . . .

Sophia was touched that both her uncle and aunt should have taken the trouble to come to Cheltenham station to meet her; it seemed surprising that they should endow her visit with any significance. There was the inevitable awkwardness of a first meeting after two years but her aunt was never short of words for long. 'Harry's got a motor car,' she said. 'It's so useful for a country doctor, though he's always getting it stuck on farm tracks. He won't learn.' Sophia was moved by the warmth of her aunt's embrace and the brightness of her smile. She reflected suddenly that Needlewick must be a dull and lonely place for her aunt now that her daughter Helen had left and her best friend, Eleanor Gresham, was dead.

The women sat crushed together in the back of the car, the flow of Margaret's conversation unimpeded by the noise of the engine. Sophia leaned against the hard seat and watched the high-banked lanes jolt past. How clearly she remember her former visit: the trip from the station in an open trap through drizzle, the sharp pain at the base of her neck as her collar was soaked through and the sense of dragging despair as the chestnut horses pulled her further and further from the station, from Nicholas and from her mother.

'I thought I'd come to the station,' her aunt said. 'I had some shopping in Cheltenham. It's so unlike Harry to offer to bring me. You know, Sophia, we were thrilled to hear of your engagement. Lady Kilbride sounds very grand, doesn't it? How will you like being called that? I wish Helen would marry. She's getting old now, twenty-four. Well, of course I know you're a year older and the war came – so many young men . . . But it seems odd for her to be with all those women.'

'How is Helen?' Sophia shouted. 'I'm longing to hear all about her. She sounds quite brilliant.'

'Oh she is. But it's a strange life for a girl. I keep hoping she'll decide to be a teacher after all and come back to a local school. But she doesn't seem to want to leave Cambridge. I say Harry, do watch these bends. He drives so fast.'

Her feminine conversation was restful to Sophia who studied her aunt for some resemblance to her mother but found none except in the shape of nose and chin. Aunt Margaret was quite plump and still incurably untidy, modern clothes did not become her at all and brown had never suited her. Her hair was still worn in an untidy chignon with the inevitable wispy grey strands escaping from under her hat.

Harry had a call to make in Needlewick and wondered if the ladies would mind walking to Roundstones from the village – he'd bring the luggage later. This was not what Sophia had planned, she had wanted her first walk through this place charged with memory to be alone, not with chattering Aunt Margaret, but she said: 'Of course I shall enjoy the walk. And I'm so looking forward to seeing Roundstones again.'

He dropped them at the bottom of the High Street. 'I expect you'll notice plenty of changes, Sophia. Even Needlewick cannot quite escape the modern world.'

Sophia was disappointed. Despite her unpropitiously damp arrival in that summer of 1909, her imagination had retained a picture of Needlewick floating like a watercolour in an eternal mist of hot blue days. But on this cloudy May afternoon of her return it seemed an unremarkable little village distinguished only by its fine Norman church on the hill. The surface of the High Street had been repaired, the chickens had gone from the yard of the Makepeace cottage and near the church stood a new white cenotaph.

'It seems much smaller, things always do,' she said, shivering. 'And it was always so hot when I was here last.'

'We've had some lovely days this spring. We can't really complain.'

'That's where the Makepeace family lived, isn't it? Are they still there?'

'Some. Two of the boys were killed in the war – another came back not quite right. One of the girls is married, another in service. There are only two at home now.'

'Were there only six? There seemed to be hundreds of children.'

'There were others. Some died. We had a spate of infant deaths in the village before the war – your uncle suspected the water.'

Makepeace children ought not to die, ought not to grow up and fight in wars. They stand forever in cottage doorways, extending filthy hands for raspberry drops and grinning toothily at well-dressed visitors from London.

The two women crossed the bridge and began to climb towards Roundstones. 'Does Mrs Bubb still work for you?' asked Sophia.

'Oh good heavens yes, she's a dear. I couldn't manage without her.'

'I'm afraid she and I didn't quite see eye to eye when I was last here.'

'Oh, I don't know. You were only a child.'

They had just rounded a slight bend. Sophia stopped. A man sat on a gate beside the lane, stripping the seeds from a sheaf of grasses. He smiled at her. 'Michael!' she cried.

He doffed his cap but did not get off the gate. Her aunt took her elbow and ushered her along. 'I expect Mrs Bubb will have steak and kidney pudding for supper, we usually have steak and kidney on a Thursday.' Margaret spoke in a high, loud voice until they were well out of earshot. 'You remember him then?' she whispered at last.

'Yes. He used to work for Uncle Harry, didn't he? I'd recognise him anywhere. Does he still work at Roundstones?'

'Oh no!'

'I was surprised to see him. I would have thought he'd be the sort to get away as soon as possible.'

'He's never left Needlewick.'

'Not even in the war?'

'He wasn't called up – medical reasons. Instead he stayed here, working as a labourer. They were all desperate for men. I should keep out of his way, Sophia. He's a bit odd. It's said he watches people in a very unpleasant manner. Girls. You know what I mean.'

Sophia, who was struck suddenly by a vivid memory of Michael from of old, could not help thinking that he was a very minor threat compared to the type of man she occasionally encountered in London.

But now they could see Roundstones tucked into the hillside, its oriel window blindly reflecting the afternoon sunshine. 'I had forgotten what a lovely house it is!' Sophia said. 'And the view!' They paused to look down the valley towards the Needle. 'Is the bridge still there? And the path by the river?'

'You do have a good memory. Yes, the path's probably overgrown now. I don't use it much. The road's so much more convenient for the village.'

But the path Sophia remembered went in another direction.

'I expect you could do with a cup of tea. Come in, dear. We've put you in the room you had before. I always leave Helen's free in case she might drop by on impulse. Mrs Bubb. We're back.'

Sophia knew from her previous visit that bells were never rung in Roundstones. If Mrs Bubb's services were required, Helen or Aunt Margaret used to creep down to the kitchen, knock on the door and murmur: 'I'm sorry to disturb you, Mrs Bubb, but would you mind . . .'

And here she was, lumbering along the passage, skirts fractionally shorter, hair thinner but otherwise little changed.

'Good afternoon, Mrs Bubb!' Sophia cried. 'I've been so looking forward to seeing you again!' The words splintered at her feet as Mrs Bubb eyed her scornfully and said: 'I've set the tea in the drawing-room.' Sophia had no illusions about the housekeeper's opinion of her: over-dressed, over-indulged, indolent and affected.

But despite Mrs Bubb's hostility Sophia was content: the smell of Roundstones, fresh green scent from the gardens, beeswax, old books, stone flags; the cool dim rooms; the hot tea and wonderful, thickly buttered scones; her aunt's interminable flow of observations and questions; all was as it should be.

I was happy here, Sophia thought, until the end, and I didn't realise. I have not been happy since. I cried and suffered here, but at least I was alive, at least I felt. I have not felt anything so acutely since – even mother's leaving and Nicholas's death seemed to happen at a distance. Here everything was so immediate, or perhaps it was because I was a child then, and have since grown up.

'You must tell me about your plans, all your wonderful news,' said Margaret. 'I was so flattered, Sophia, that you should spare the time to come to Needlewick before your marriage.'

Sophia was too ashamed of the years she had neglected the family at Needlewick to mention Mr Gresham's letter. 'Yes, I felt I must come back. I'm sorry I never made time before.'

'Oh, we wouldn't expect it! You've been far too busy – your poor father must have needed you, a great comfort to him . . .' Margaret skimmed away from naming her sister Suzanna, the one who always hovered, phantom-like, behind a mention of Simon Theobald. 'So tell me about your fiancé. What's it like to be engaged to a lord?'

In this drawing-room, with its old chintz and polished boards, Sophia had yawned through so many tea-times, studied each volume on the shelves in the hope of finding amusement, sat apparently absorbed by letters from home in the hope that her preoccupation would ward off Mrs Bubb's attempt to involve her in the housework. Boredom is such a luxury, she reflected, a simple discomfort. I wish now I was only bored, then I wouldn't have to lie to Colin.

'I suppose I don't think much about the title,' she said.

'Of course. I'm so silly. How trivial you must think me. Forgive me.'

'Colin's very good to me, much more than I deserve. I'm afraid he spoils me.'

'That's as it should be. I remember when your uncle and I were engaged he'd always bring me something; flowers, a card, a book.'

It was strange to imagine gentle Aunt Margaret in the throes of a love affair. Colin had never brought Sophia a little posy or chosen a book for her. His presents were lavish; a sheaf of carnations, Swiss chocolates, silk. 'I sometimes wish he wouldn't,' she admitted, and then made an extraordinary admission – to her aunt, of all people. 'Aunt Margaret, sometimes I wonder if I'm right to marry him.'

Margaret laughed: 'All girls have qualms before they marry. After all, it's a big step. You must be sure. Have you chosen a dress?'

There was no help then. Sophia let the moment pass. 'I'm very fond of ivory. And my mother carried white flowers. So shall I.'

'Yes, I remember. I have a photograph in a drawer here. Would you like to see it? Oh Suzanna was so beautiful on her wedding day.' Before Sophia could resist, a photograph was placed in her hands and there was her mother in a cascade of satin and net, waist pinched, eyes huge under piled hair and a streaming veil. And beside her chair stood Simon Theobald, slender, upright, gripping her shoulder.

'When I was here before,' said Sophia, 'you used to display this photograph on the bookcase.'

'So I did. But since your mother . . . I didn't want to upset you . . .'

Ranked on either side of the wedding couple were Suzanna's relatives and friends; Margaret herself under a hat so large only her chin was visible, Mrs Deborah Parditer in a blouse with a fearsome bow, her sister, Lady Jane Middlecote, amidst a flutter of apologetic lace and yes, Eleanor Gresham, youthful and soft-haired but with that customary quizzical expression in her eyes.

'You all look so young,' exclaimed Sophia.

'We *were* young. And now your mother is gone and dear Eleanor Gresham is dead. Eleanor has died. Oh, of course you know. I miss her so, she was my dearest friend.'

'I felt very sad for Mr Gresham when he came to London.'

'Yes, poor man. He's managed so well. They knew for years that she was very sick, but they never said a word, not even to Harry.'

Sophia could not bear to dwell on Mrs Gresham's suffering. 'And Helen? You must be so proud of her.'

'Oh we are. She has done wonderfully well for a girl.'

'Do you visit her often?'

'Occasionally. But she's so busy. I never could have imagined Helen in one of those places. Of course I can't begin to take in what it is she studies. Mathematics always seemed such an odd choice for her. She loved pictures and stories when she was a very little girl.'

'I would like to see her again. We hardly spoke at Nicholas's funeral.'

'You had other things to think about then, dear, we understood.'

'I wrote and told her I was going to be married. She didn't reply.'

'I expect she didn't have time. She's always so busy. So many books, students . . .'

The doctor's voice could be heard in the kitchen.

'I'll go and help with my bag,' Sophia said, 'and have a wash.'

'Yes, how selfish of me to keep you talking after your journey.' Margaret began to collect the tea things.

Sophia met her uncle in the hall and took her luggage from him. He looked very weary.

'That's right, don't let him carry them heavy bags. You go and sit down, Doctor, I'll bring a cup of tea.' Mrs Bubb chivvied him into the drawing-room and Sophia slowly climbed the stairs. On her way along the landing she passed the closed door of Helen's room and then came to the spare room which was even more cluttered than she remembered. It had obviously become the repository for old books, knick-knacks and unwanted items of furniture. The coverlet was glaringly modern, a loud floral pattern, probably purchased at a garden party. There were flowers on the bedside table.

She went at once to the window looking out over the garden. There was the little gate and beyond the wall the willow tree by the river. The greyness of the afternoon and the attractive but unremarkable view almost made her weep because it held none of the enchantment endowed by memory. No Helen in a grimy flounced pinafore stood on the terrace calling Sophia's name, there was no invitation to shared secrets under the willow.

A small mirror stood on the chest-of-drawers and in it Sophia caught a glimpse of her trim, adult form. We had such lovely clothes in those days, she thought, or at least I did, not poor Helen, who was dressed in cast-offs and peculiar home-made frocks. Mine were all tucked and embroidered and starched. She smiled, remembering Mrs Bubb's opinion of those creations when they had to be laundered. Now Mrs Bubb – she had not changed. She at least was constant. Listening, Sophia could hear the housekeeper's heavy tread on the stairs, otherwise house and garden were quiet. A blackbird on the lawn cocked its head. The wind lifted the skirts of the willow.

4

Sophia had not expected it to rain in Needlewick. Throughout her previous visit the weather had been almost entirely dry and warm so that the lanes were crisply rutted with dry mud the colour of Helen's hair and cows had steamed in the parched field, pestered by flies. The only times it rained were the day of her arrival and during a wedding when thunder had ricocheted through the church with such force that the candles flickered.

She had therefore forgotten how small and dark Roundstones was, how little there would be to do. How had she stuck it before? With bad grace, she imagined, although at least then she'd had Helen for company. Now there was only Aunt Margaret, determined to entertain her guest whilst obviously in a fidget to get on with her usual Friday routine.

'Aunt, please let me help you clear the table,' Sophia said after breakfast.

'No, I won't hear of it, you are on holiday. I'll just take these to the kitchen for Mrs Bubb and then we'll go to the drawing-room. I have a few photographs of Helen you might like to see – there's one of her graduation.'

'Let me load the tray. I remember Mrs Bubb was

annoyed with me when I was here before, all pampered and refusing to lift a finger.'

They laughed a little self-consciously.

'She does look remarkably well,' Sophia added. 'I always thought of her as really old, the way one does as a child, but she seems just the same now as then. But she was housekeeper here when you and mama were children, wasn't she?'

'She's part of Roundstones and she doesn't change though perhaps she's slowed up. I'll just take these through now. Please, Sophia, you go and sit down.'

Sophia wandered across the hall to the drawing-room where the windows overlooked the dripping garden. So much for nostalgic rambles, for communing with the lost days of her childhood and finding solace in the quiet valley of the Needle.

But by lunch-time she was ready to ignore the weather. Aunt Margaret was a good companion for an hour, tedious for longer. Sophia was longing for her mother's name to be spoken, for her aunt to indulge in childhood reminiscences or to discuss Helen but apparently there were to be no confidences, only chat about the forthcoming flower festival and fête, and the state of Harry's medical practice. Margaret of course wanted to hear about Sophia's wedding plans but at Roundstones, cloaked by rain, the wedding seemed to Sophia a mere pinprick at the wrong end of a telescope; the marriage of another Sophia, a smart, London Sophia who didn't yawn achingly behind her hand at ten o'clock in the morning or remember with a peculiar twist of the heart the row of books in the glass case which had not changed in eleven years. I know, she realised suddenly, that, if I reach for the one with green binding third from the left, it will be *The Wide, Wide World.*

'I think I must go for a walk this afternoon – regardless of the rain,' Sophia said at lunch.

'But it's pouring. I'm sure it will be better tomorrow. And Jane Middlecote said she might call this afternoon.'

'I'll be back by four. I don't mind the rain, really. Lovely clean country rain, so unlike the murk of London.'

'Well you must take my galoshes and you can have Harry's old umbrella. Where will you go?'

'I thought down to the river and into Needlewick across the fields. I'll call on Mr Gresham.'

'Oh yes, for the diary. Fancy Eleanor leaving you that. So strange. I can't understand why she thought you would want Helen's childish scribblings.'

'Would you like to see it?' Sophia asked gently.

'Oh no, no. I won't delve into the past, such a foolish thing to do. Live in the present, that's what I say.'

'I'm sure it's safer.' Sophia took the umbrella and even obediently donned the galoshes before leaving Round-stones by the garden door. The rain was soft, a caress, and the air lush with the scent of grass and sodden flowers. When she came to the willow, a fountain of wet leaves, she parted the branches and peered into the green cave within.

The path beside the river meandered upstream, muddy and uninviting. That way lay the Tunnel Woods. Sophia turned hurriedly and made for the little footbridge and the path up the valley towards Middlecote Hall.

The rain had grown heavier by the time she reached

the village so she paid a reluctant visit to the church. But in the porch she found her way barred by a pair of outstretched legs. They were not moved to let her pass and their owner, who was lolling on a narrow stone bench, said: 'I thought you'd remember me. I never forgot you. I knew you'd come back one day.'

Sophia tried to keep her voice steady. 'Goodness! How are you, Michael?'

'Oh not so bad.'

'I was just on my way to visit Mr Gresham.'

'He's not in. He rarely is on a weekday afternoon any more.'

'Ah – well, never mind.'

Now that she had the chance to study him more closely she saw that Michael was still very small, thin-faced and bony, even less prepossessing as an adult than as a child. Already, although he could only have been in his mid-twenties, his hair was thinning and his pronounced teeth discoloured.

'Staying long, are you?' he asked.

'Not very, no.'

She wanted to escape but could not step over his legs and was too proud to retreat without an excuse. 'I'll try Mr Gresham and then I really must be getting back to Roundstones.'

He stood up and fell in beside her. 'What have you been doing all these years?'

'Oh, growing up. I'm engaged,' she told him desperately. 'And you?'

'Much the same.' He held the lych-gate open, forcing her to walk very close to him as she passed through.

'Well, I mustn't keep you,' she said.

'I've nothing else on. I don't often get the chance to speak to the bride-to-be of a lord.'

How did he know about Colin? They came to The Grey House, where Mr Gresham's servant, a newcomer, said he was out but was expecting Sophia to call, perhaps on Saturday. When she turned back to the road, Michael had gone.

As Sophia walked rapidly down the High Street she wondered what Michael wanted with her – he could not be trusted to have a simple motive; he had been a frightening child given to lurking close at hand and appearing at unlikely moments. Such was the force of one particular memory that Sophia stumbled, as if caught in a gust of wind. She could see, clearly, Michael's boyish hand and grubby face, there in the clearing, in the leaves, and Helen's body rigid, her face transfixed.

They were waiting for her in the drawing-room: Aunt Margaret, Lady Jane Middlecote whose strangely neutral quality Sophia remembered well, and a heavy-chested woman with eager, inquiring eyes. Jarred by her recent encounter, Sophia was caught off balance by the current of expectation in the room and her usually assured smile was shaky.

'Ah, here she is at last!' cried Aunt Margaret, ushering her into the room and touching her hair. 'I hope you didn't get too wet. I was telling them I couldn't keep you indoors.'

'Lady Middlecote. How lovely to see you again.' Sophia's voice, at least, was controlled.

Lady Middlecote shook her hand, kissed her cheek and introduced her sister, Mrs Deborah Parditer, who said: 'You won't recognise me, of course, but you came to my daughter's wedding. I remember you well. I see you've fined down – don't get as thin as your mother. And you've resisted the temptation to cut your hair.'

'Oh yes,' Sophia replied, ignoring the intimacy of Mrs Parditer's last comments, 'I remember, there was a thunderstorm. Is your daughter well?'

'Very. She has three children of her own now.'

'And you, Sophia? You are to be married. We were all so pleased to hear the news,' said Lady Middlecote, embracing Sophia once more in her soft arms and bosom. 'I always knew you were destined for great things. I remember you handing out the prizes at our garden party, so composed and magnanimous for so young a girl.'

'It is Helen who has been successful,' Sophia said. 'I have merely found a wealthy husband. She must have worked terribly hard – for a woman she's done extremely well, don't you think?'

'Your father must be very pleased,' said Mrs Parditer obviously determined that the subject of Sophia's marriage should not yet be dismissed.

'He is. Very. I'm a fortunate young lady,' replied Sophie coolly.

'And what does your mother think?'

'You must be more than ready for tea, Sophia,' interrupted Margaret. 'Are you sure you're not damp – perhaps you should change your shoes?'

'They're quite dry. I wore your galoshes and, unlike

35

last time I was here, I came properly equipped with strong shoes. My mother has not written for some time,' Sophia added, returning Mrs Parditer's direct gaze. 'I was wondering whether she might have written to one of you? Or perhaps Mrs Gresham? I know they were very close at one time.'

Lady Middlecote, whose eyes had met Margaret's, seized the opportunity to change the subject. 'Of course you've heard of our loss. Our dear friend. But I believe she left you something in her will.'

Sophia realised wearily that everyone in Needlewick must know about the diary. 'Yes, I'm amazed she remembered me.'

'Eleanor would never forget anyone. She was very wise, such a loss to us all.'

There was a pause and then Aunt Margaret said: 'You see, Sophia, she was an invalid for so long and towards the end reading or sewing or even talking tired her. It's no wonder some of her ideas were a little strange – she had so many hours of enforced inactivity.'

'Do you suppose she was ill, even when I was in Needlewick all those years ago?'

'Oh yes, she knew long before then.'

Sophia remembered Mrs Gresham on her bicycle, free wheeling, light dress flying, hair loosened beneath her hat. 'She used to ride a bicycle,' she murmured.

'Yes, she loved that machine. She gave it to Helen before the war when she had to give up riding it.'

'Poor John,' sighed Lady Middlecote. 'Poor man! He was devoted to her.'

Margaret, who seemed to find this conversation

particularly painful, began to fuss about the tea: 'Mrs Bubb is very late. I'll go and help, I know she's been busy spring cleaning in the scullery.'

'No, let me, I insist. You sit still, Aunt!' Sophia could not stand the scrutiny of Mrs Parditer and her sister any longer. She was an invader in such a tight little group that she felt consumed by their craving for novelty. Placing her hands on her aunt's shoulders, she pressed her firmly back into the chair, and escaped.

'Oh she's so beautiful,' murmured Jane Middlecote the instant the door was closed, 'I never thought she would be such a beauty.'

'She's nothing like her mother,' said Deborah, 'she has none of Suzanna's delicacy.'

'But she's so much easier now. She's lost all her little airs and graces. She doesn't seem to mind how homely we are here,' Margaret said.

'She seems very reluctant to talk about her wedding,' remarked Deborah. 'Hardly my idea of the blushing bride.'

'Girls are so much more sophisticated now, not like us.'

'Does she say much about her mother, Margaret?'

'I don't like to bring up the subject of Suzanna. I know her father wouldn't like it, and I feel I'd inevitably be taking sides.'

'You mean *you* can't bear to mention Suzanna's name! You'd be doing the girl a great favour, she must be missing her a good deal at present. A girl needs her mother when she is to be married. Not that Suzanna would be any help, I admit.'

'Hush, Deborah, please!'

'Oh for goodness sake!' Deborah straightened in her chair and turned away her head. 'I'm surprised the peonies aren't out, Margaret. They're late, aren't they?' Thoughts of Suzanna, and of Suzanna's daughter Sophia with her steady dark eyes and forced smile were so unsettling.

'Yes, they're late, everything is.'

This safe topic was seized on with enthusiasm and when Sophia came back, prettily flushed by the unaccustomed task of carrying a laden tray, the three were harmoniously discussing the proper method of dealing with slugs.

5

The air on a mild May morning in Needlewick was soupy with the perfume of thrusting blossom and fresh green leaves. Beyond the garden of Middlecote Hall the water-meadow was hedged with hawthorn, elder and knee-high nettles. Cows browsed near the river, still, at six-thirty, a little stupid from the cool of the night.

It was ages since Deborah Parditer had been down to the river so early, not indeed since her wedding morning some thirty-five years ago, but she had woken at four and for once been unable to harness sleep or drifting thoughts. A blackbird sang persistently outside her window and in the eaves the youthful contents of a starling's nest hawked so relentlessly for food that she at last got up, dressed, and let herself out of the Hall.

But here by the river she found no peace. Here, the ghost of Suzanna Gilling, with long blonde hair neatly plaited under a straw boater, seemed to hang over the little wooden bridge with her sister Margaret and drop sticks into the water, hers, as always first and fastest.

'Go on, Margaret! Throw yours. You're too slow! Let it go with the current!'

Then across the water was the willow where the five of them, The Needlewick Five as they secretly designated themselves, held their meetings, planned their tea parties and wrote their magazine.

Deborah, then Deborah Henshaw, always kept the minutes which began with a list of 'Those Present' August 6, 1878, and continued with 'Apologies for Absence'. For years there were seldom Apologies, and then more and more often: Suzanna Gilling . . .

Next came the Officers' Reports – each girl held an Office, even little Jane Henshaw. First Suzanna, the Chairman, spoke – since she had invented the club she must be its driving force and organiser. Her report dwelt on past achievements and future pleasures: 'We are pleased to report that Eleanor Carney has embarked on the study of Latin with her father the Reverend James Carney and can already decline the verb to love . . . (Go on Eleanor, let's hear . . .) Jane and Deborah Henshaw have completed their samplers; we regret that Jane's is rather grubby, but know she will do better next time. Despite Deborah's incessant moans she has as usual achieved perfection. Margaret – what have you been up to, Meg? – Oh yes, her radishes didn't go woody this year . . . And I – I have completed the Brontë novels and am about to start on Mrs Gaskell.

'As a society The Needlewick Five left surprise food parcels for three villagers and [lowered voice] actually achieved its long-held ambition to meet at midnight under the willow [giggles]. For future plans see "Any Other Business". Yes, I've got a wonderful idea, but first, the Treasurer's report. Margaret?'

Out came Margaret's pocket book, carefully ruled, every farthing meticulously entered or subtracted. It was a rule that each girl should contribute half her pocket money.

Eleanor was 'Village Affairs Correspondent'. 'The main event was the wedding of George Makepeace, aged twenty, to Ellen Greene, aged sixteen, on Saturday 26 April. The bride wore a pale grey gown in sprigged cotton and carried primroses. The Needlewick Five gathered at the lych-gate to throw rice . . .'

Secretary – Deborah. 'No letters received, but one sent to Mrs Bubb at Roundstones thanking her for her kind culinary contribution to the April picnic . . .'

'Honorary President, that's you, Jane – nothing to report? Good, then on to "Any Other Business". Now then, the May picnic – the Tunnel Woods!'

'But Suzanna, we went there last year!'

'I know. But this year' . . . dramatic pause . . . 'we're going *into* the tunnel.'

Mrs Deborah Parditer, formerly Deborah Henshaw, secretary to The Needlewick Five, stood on the footbridge and gazed upstream towards those same Tunnel Woods.

Suzanna would not be kept away from them. Needlewick, set in a valley, was close to so much woodland that trees, bluebells, ferns, woodland paths held no special allure for The Needlewick Five. The Henshaw girls rode daily and were so familiar with the area that they could have been carried blindfold down overgrown paths and known precisely where to duck their heads. But they never rode to the Tunnel Woods which were, besides being private property, too dark and steep to attract girls on horseback.

However, The Needlewick Five went there one year, as a result of Suzanna's lust for novelty, when Deborah, the eldest, was thirteen and Jane, the youngest, seven. Suzanna, as usual, had got her way by fielding their objections with a quick smile and deft retorts none of them could resist. First the cool-headed but devoted Eleanor would be coaxed on to her side, then sister Margaret and finally the reluctant, and, in Deborah's case, sulky, Henshaw girls. And to the Tunnel Woods they went.

They had, in previous years, picnicked by the river and clambered up a steep path through the trees until they came to the mouth of a tunnel, a folly, Mrs Bubb had later informed them, cut through the rock by a previous owner with a taste for the Gothic. But, although they returned several times, the girls had never ventured inside the tunnel. It was too dark, too narrow, and always a little too late to explore further.

But now, when Suzanna said, 'And this time we will go *into* the tunnel,' a thrill had passed through the group because go they would, following Suzanna's trim, determined figure, up the steep path and into the tunnel and heaven knew what mysteries and excitement, and there could be no turning back.

And who could say, Mrs Deborah Parditer now thought, if things might have turned out better or worse without that trip to the Tunnel Woods with two baskets of food – chicken sandwiches and apples packed at Roundstones – and their strongest shoes?

Suzanna had sung: *Where are you going to my pretty maid?* and took little bouncing skips on the chorus, '*Sir, she said, Sir, she said* . . . Come on, girls, join in!' The river was clear and quick and the sun hot on their gloved hands.

Suzanna would have drifted away anyway, Deborah now acknowledged, we could not hold her. She made too many demands that we could never satisfy.

And now the daughter, Sophia, was at Roundstones, waking in her mother's old room. What did she hope to find in Needlewick?

The clock in the tower of St John's struck the quarter, time to breakfast. Jane would not be up yet and Deborah didn't much relish Sir George's company; he would slurp his tea and attempt conversation when he had much better be silent. But she was too hungry to wait any longer.

6

At breakfast on Saturday there was a note for Sophia from Mr Gresham inviting her to call on him in The Grey House at eleven o'clock.

'I'm sure you need not go today Sophia,' Aunt Margaret said. 'I wondered if you'd like a drive, Harry's free this morning. You could go one evening perhaps.'

Sophia would not be put off – the diary was waiting for her – she could almost hear it calling, and she could not resist.

The morning was dazzling and already the warm air was full of the sickly scent of cow-parsley. There was so much space and light here that Sophia wondered why she had neglected to come back before. But really her sense of freedom was due to the fact that she was at last alone. No man pursued her activities, neither her father nor Colin. She skipped, swinging her arms, lifting her pale face to the sunshine.

The High Street was quite lively for Needlewick and Sophia smiled benignly at curious faces. She recognised none of them, though probably most knew who she was. When she came to the little lane which led to The Grey House the memory of the hot garden wall, smelling softly of stone and earth, was so powerful that she thought: If I enter quietly by the garden door I will find Mrs Gresham seated under the apple tree.

But the garden was empty and overgrown and Mr Gresham stood in the french windows, waiting for her.

'It's in my study,' he said at once. 'We'll fetch it.'

The house was very still and a masculine gloom had settled. Eleanor had died and with her delicacy and brightness. Mr Gresham and Sophia did not speak as they crossed the hall as if in fear of waking a sleeping child.

His study was a dark, north-facing room; with a sudden flash of understanding Sophia realised that he had probably chosen it so that his wife could sit in the light room facing the garden. Shelves were laden with legal volumes, quarterly magazines and haphazard piles of papers. On the desk was a wedding photograph, Mrs Gresham in a white, voluminous dress, he standing to attention behind her.

'Eleanor never let me take any photographs,' Mr Gresham said softly. 'This is all I have.'

'Why ever not?'

'She wouldn't have me record her slow decline but thought my memories would be enough. Perhaps she was right. Here is the diary. It seems hardly worth your coming all this way.'

There were two cheap red exercise books, well thumbed. On the covers, in faded ink, was carefully inscribed the name: *Helen Margaret Callwood*.

'There were others, earlier ones, I believe, but my wife only kept these.'

Tucked into one was a slip of paper on which was

scrawled, as if with a damaged pen: '*For Sophia. Don't forget. From Eleanor Gresham, February 1920.*'

'Surely, Mr Gresham, this note is for you,' Sophia exclaimed.

'No, she told me to give it to you. She was very particular about all the things she left – she had lots of time to plan, you see.'

They stood awkwardly by the desk, then he said hurriedly: 'I expect you're in a rush to get back to the Round House, but it's so hot, perhaps you'd like a glass of lemonade, or sherry?'

She could not leave him to his lonely Saturday morning. 'That would be lovely. Perhaps in the garden? I've never forgotten your garden.'

He disappeared down a passage to the kitchen leaving Sophia to wonder why Needlewick residents were always so afraid of their servants.

The garden had of course shrunk. She remembered it as boundless but now it seemed to have closed in on itself, huddled up. She found Mrs Gresham's little paved walk to the rose garden where many of the blooms were overblown and the leaves blighted.

Mr Gresham appeared with two glasses. 'I'm afraid I know nothing about gardening,' he said. 'We have a man who comes a couple of times a week but it doesn't seem to be enough.' He set the glasses down carefully on the edge of the garden seat. 'I hope this bench won't mark your frock.'

'Oh, it's only an old thing!' she said, safe in the knowledge that he would be ignorant of London fashion.

They sat awkwardly with the diary between them. 'Have you read it?' she asked.

He gave her a quick glance. 'Not recently. I believe I did have a look when Helen first gave it to my wife – long before the war.'

'I wonder how Helen came to give away something so personal.'

He gripped his hands in his lap. 'Helen stopped visiting us so often, you know. Eleanor was very sorry. And then she went away to school.'

'Helen always used to love coming to this house.'

'She grew tired of Needlewick. I suppose any intelligent young person would.'

'Do you remember what you read in the diary?'

Another pause. 'My head has been filled with so many facts since then.'

After a moment Sophia asked: 'Shall you go on living here, Mr Gresham?' She was watching his hands, still folded firmly, as if he were afraid they would make some desperate gesture if he freed them. He seemed to Sophia the most fragile human being she had ever known, as if grief had thinned his skin and made his bones brittle.

'I don't know, it's such a short while since she died. At the moment I couldn't bear to leave – not when I remember her so vividly. And the summer is worse – I had not expected . . . She loved the sunshine and the garden.'

Sophia said nothing. Then she surprised herself by putting her hand on Mr Gresham's. 'I'm sure she was very happy with you.'

'She always said so, she always said I made her happy.' And he gave Sophia a look so filled with sorrow that she

47

had to swallow tears. They sat in silence for a while longer, her hand on his cold fingers.

'I'm afraid I must go now,' she said at last. 'I'm expected back for lunch.'

'Of course. I apologise. I didn't mean to keep you. Thank you.'

'It is I who should thank you for keeping these note-books safe for me when you have so much else on your mind. Goodbye, Mr Gresham.'

'Goodbye, Sophia.'

He walked with her to the gate and as she left him in the empty garden, she reflected that she had just passed one of the most difficult half hours of her life, but at the same time the most surprising. In the moment when she had reached out her hand and touched his, she had acted with more spontaneity than she had ever known.

In the afternoon she developed a bad headache – so desperate was she to avoid her aunt's plans for tea at Middlecote Hall that the pain became real. 'I must lie down, Aunt Margaret. I'm so sorry, the sunshine this morning was too much, I expect. My hat hasn't much of a brim.'

Margaret was no fool. She had noticed Sophia's bul-ging pocket when she came back at lunch-time, how she had carried her jacket hurriedly upstairs, and her con-fusion when she answered enquiries about Mr Gresham's health.

At three Margaret left Roundstones to take tea at the Hall. The doctor was away on a call so Sophia was alone.

Stifled by the silent house – Mrs Bubb had gone upstairs to rest in her room on the attic floor – Sophia took the diaries down to the willow where the afternoon sun was diffused by the curtain of leaves. Bathed in mellow green light, she began to read.

7

Helen Margaret Callwood

HER DIARY

WEDNESDAY, 14 JULY 1909

There was another letter from Aunt Suzanna this morning. Nicholas is far worse. Father said that measles are really very common and most people survive any complications, but mother said my cousin may go blind. I believe she secretly thinks he'll die. Of course we've never met Nicholas at all but his death would cause such sadness in the family, he's so young.

And Sophia will arrive tomorrow by the three o'clock train. I have been sitting under the hawthorn tree all afternoon thinking about her. Up until now I have been unable to grasp that she might actually come. How strange it will be to share my summer. I have no idea what she is like, she is a dream figure to me. All I really know about her is that she is my cousin, has a dying brother and very rich parents.

I have two imaginary pictures of her. One is that she'll be rather like a porcelain statue, delicate, but cold. She will sit all day at the piano and hardly speak to me. The other is that she will love me and be as anxious as I am to be friends. What a perfect summer we would have then.

I'm really terribly nervous about her. All afternoon my thoughts have swung from one possibility to another. Half of me says, she'll ruin my summer, Needlewick is mine, I don't want to share it, she'll cut me off from my people. The other half replies: yes, but you may love her, you may find you want to give her everything and then I start planning our days together. I'll show her Needlewick and the willow and the church. We'll visit Mrs Gresham and the Middlecotes and go to the garden party. I'll have a friend for the first time, someone to share things with, even, possibly, maybe, my people? Could I?

In the end I forced myself to be quiet. I sat under the hawthorn tree making the most of my last chance of being alone there as I am now – Helen on her own. I needed to see my people to tell them what's happening but they didn't come. Even though it was damp they should have come. They must have known I needed them.

I felt sad as I left the clearing. I had looked forward to so many long afternoons there this summer. But now, because of Sophia, I shan't be free to visit when I wish.

I am so muddled and nervous.

In twenty-four hours Sophia will be here. How will I be feeling then?

FRIDAY, 16 JULY 1909
Cousin Sophia has been here a day now. She has changed everything. The house even smells different because she is here.

Yesterday I woke early. Even in my sleep I must have

51

known and remembered she was coming. When I saw the rain I was sad because she would not first see Needle-wick in the sunshine. Mother and Mrs Bubb and I were run off our feet all morning. Mother said that Sophia is used to such comfort and elegance that Roundstones will be a shock to her. How could anyone dislike Roundstones?

I prepared her room. She has new muslin curtains and the cushion I've been embroidering in brown and gold cross-stitch is on the bed. I put out the best towels and picked flowers, all the sweetest smelling. I can't think that she could be used to anything quite so comfortable and elegant as her room then looked.

Mrs Bubb did not seem very excited. In fact, when I was helping her cut scones in the kitchen she was more ill-tempered than usual. 'It'll do that girl the world of good to be out of town, away from all those servants swarming around,' she told me. 'She'll be spoilt to death, I expect. I daresay she'll hardly even know how to dress herself.'

'But she'll be dreadfully homesick,' I said. I thought Mrs Bubb ought to be sorry for Sophia. It must be terrible to leave home for three weeks.

'Nonsense, she'll be as hard as nails.'

At last when everything was ready, even the supper table laid, I managed to get away. I had to make a last effort to see my people before Sophia arrived even though it was very wet outside. Everything seemed to be espe-cially green and strong in the woods by the stream because she was coming. Each time I passed one of my favourite spots, I thought of how next time I would perhaps be with Sophia.

My people did not come, I don't know why I expected them. They so dislike the rain. I left a sign that I had been and came home.

As soon as I opened the kitchen door I sensed that Sophia had arrived. I did not wait to remove my coat, I could not. I ran upstairs and knocked on her bedroom door.

She is beautiful, my cousin. She is only fourteen but seems far more than a year older than me. She was sitting on the bed with one hand lying on my cushion, wearing the softest pink dress, low-waisted and trimmed with ribbons and broderie anglaise. She has dark thick hair which lay smoothly on her shoulders, and tiny strap shoes. She smiled at me, got up very gracefully and shook hands.

I don't know what I said. I was too nervous and felt awkward standing there with my wet hair. She was thoughtful, like an adult. She told me to go and dry myself. At supper she was very polite but quiet. She has a small appetite and nibbled at some toast. Mother talked mostly, asking after Aunt Suzanna and Uncle Simon and poor Cousin Nicholas. She told Sophia how ill I had once been with measles and about when I had mumps. It made me feel silly but Sophia didn't mind at all, kept smiling politely.

She was very tired and went to bed soon after the meal. She did not get up until ten this morning. Mrs Bubb wanted me to go and call her in time for breakfast but mother said I should take up tea on a tray instead. Sophia has the most beautiful nightgown with rows of lace in the neck and sleeves.

It has rained all day. I showed Sophia my room this morning and suggested she might like to look at my books and dolls. She did not seem interested in them. Of course she is too old for dolls. I am really. Also, none of my old toys is in very good condition.

I hope Sophia won't find it too quiet here. I wish the sun would shine. She asked me what I normally do on wet days during the holidays.

'I practise the piano or help Mrs Bubb and mother or read or play or study.' I could not tell her about my dreams or my private games or my people. I may never tell her. 'What about you?' I asked.

'I would not even get up until midday,' she said rather impatiently. 'And then there'd be callers or flowers to arrange or embroidery of course. Usually my brother and I go to stay with my Uncle Thomas Theobald for the summer season. He has a house on the coast.'

I don't know much about Sophia's Uncle Thomas because he's on her father's side. I asked why she had not gone to stay with him this time.

'Good gracious, I might be infectious!' she said. 'It's all right to come here, you've had the measles.'

She has gone to bed early again tonight.

I pray that the sun might shine tomorrow so I can take her into the garden and to the village. I expect she seems unhappy at the moment because she is homesick and still tired after the journey. I hope she will settle down, I like being with her so much. I just like looking at her, the detail of her, the way her hair is pulled so smoothly back from her forehead and then divides when it reaches her shoulders so that most of it lies in a straight line along her back, the tucks and buttons and lacy bits on her clothes, and how her fingernails are so clean and trim. I just hope I don't seem too childish and silly to her.

It was a mistake to think she'd be interested in dolls.

TUESDAY, 20 JULY 1909
Yesterday was warm and breezy and the sun shone. I took Sophia on a tour of Needlewick. I did not go near the tunnels or my people, of course. I still feel very nervous. She's so much more experienced than I am, our lives up until now have been so different it is hard to believe we are cousins and share the same grandparents.

We went along the lane to the village. There were still puddles from Sunday's rain and they gleamed. I walked in all the muddy bits with my thick boots so that Sophia wouldn't damage her thin shoes. Everything was very rich and bloomy. Sophia was surprised by all the butter-flies although they were only small white ones mostly. By the river near the Cheltenham road there is a mass of meadowsweet, the breeze wafted its ripe, grainy scent towards us. I love touching the fluffy heads of the flowers. Sophia says wild flowers make her sneeze. She has moved the vase out of her bedroom, I notice.

We met Michael by the river, lying on the bank spitting into the water. I introduced him to Sophia. He stood with his hands in his pockets, head down, gazing at his feet.

'This is Michael who helps father,' I told Sophia.

'Good morning, Michael,' she said in her smooth voice.

He twisted his neck sideways, squinted up at her and didn't take his eyes off her until we left. As we walked on towards the bridge, I glanced round and saw that he was still staring after us.

Sophia said: 'Helen, are you on such familiar terms with all the servants in Needlewick?'

'But he's Father's page,' I said.

'Page? Isn't that rather a grand title for an errand boy?'

'I suppose he's not a real page. We just call him that. He likes it.'

She seemed astonished. I felt a bit ashamed but I don't know what of. At the bridge I suggested we had races with sticks.

'What on earth do you mean?' she asked.

'You know, we each choose a stick, drop it in the water and then run to the other side of the bridge to see whose appears first.'

'What's the point?' she demanded.

I keep forgetting that because she's a year older than me she doesn't want to play silly games.

She was very quiet all the time. I asked her if anything was wrong. She said she was just concentrating on keeping her skirts clean.

I don't think she found much to interest her in Needlewick. She said she thought it was a cramped, dirty village and that it was a shame improvements weren't made on the cottages along the river to make them more picturesque. Apparently the inhabitants of Chelney village, which is near Chelney House, her

56

parents' country home in Hertfordshire, all have beautiful cottages. We called at the shop and I bought her some raspberry drops with my pocket money but she wouldn't eat any because she said they hurt her teeth. I told her about how ancient the inn is, but apparently my father has already given its history. I began to think she was bored with me and suggested that we might visit Mrs Gresham. Sophia said she was too tired.

Mother had given me some strawberry jam for the Makepeace family so we called on them. 'They are very poor,' I told Sophia. 'I'm afraid Mr Makepeace does not support them adequately.'

'Why ever not?'

'I believe he drinks too much.'

She looked disgusted. 'They should stop him,' she said.

When I suggested that she might like to wait outside the cottage she refused. I admire her for going in with me. All the girls were there, as well as Mrs Makepeace who is very large again. Sophia says such matters as pregnancy are not spoken of in polite circles. I wonder how the topic is avoided. Mrs Makepeace always makes me horribly awkward and I felt very foolish standing in the middle of the crowded kitchen with Sophia and a pot of jam. Through an open door I could see into the bedroom with its untidy row of mattresses. Being in the Makepeace cottage always fills me with horror. Mother says I must not get too close to the children because the insects which crawl from their hair are catching.

But the Makepeace children never look particularly miserable. There are some far poorer children in the village, although they are the biggest family. It is Mrs Makepeace who always seems so tired and ill-fed. She is so wrapped up in herself, and remote. Perhaps that's why I don't like her. She wears a grey striped dress which I believe is a cast-off from one of the servants up at Middlecote Hall. She has very large eyes, too large, and she doesn't blink as much as normal people. She frightens me with those staring eyes. I was glad Mr Makepeace wasn't at home. I dread to think what Sophia would make of him.

I introduced Sophia to Mrs Makepeace. 'This is my cousin from London. She has come to stay while her brother recovers from measles.'

She took Sophia's hand. She likes touching people. 'I hope you're not infectious,' she said. 'I don't want this lot going down with anything.'

Sophia laughed. 'I think I would have felt ill by now if I was going to have measles.'

She was very kind to Mrs Makepeace and asked the names of all the girls. We gave the children our sweets. I could see they were in awe of Sophia. She did look very beautiful in a blue dress with a white collar and her hair all loose and shiny beneath her hat. I decided that I really liked her as I watched her with those children. I think that, if she is so sympathetic, so quick to respond to children, she will understand about my people. I'd love to tell her about them so she could visit them with me. Then she wouldn't be bored. Then she'd be really interested in me.

After we left the Makepeace house, Sophia said she needed fresh air so I suggested we walk up to the church and over the hill. It was so warm and sunny we were able to sit in the meadow near the river where the Middlecote donkey is sometimes tethered. The grass is quite short there and felt dry. I picked daisies and showed Sophia how to make a chain. I asked her lots of questions about London and Aunt Suzanna and Nicholas.

'Nicholas is the best sort of brother a girl could have,' said Sophia. 'I just wish he didn't have to be at boarding school but of course he has to have a decent education. That's why it's so awful that he's ill during the summer holidays, when we are usually together.'

'What's he like?'

She bit her lip. 'He's a boy. You know, not like Michael in the village, but growing fast, and full of tricks and jokes and laughter. He stands up to father and teases me and is the only person who really makes mother smile. We're all dull without him.' She sat in the grass with her ankles crossed and her hat tipped over her eyes to shade her face. She has wonderful dark eyes but she says she hates her complexion. She says she'd rather have pink and white skin like mine. I've never thought of my skin as pink and white before. She says I should wear a larger hat to protect my nose.

After a while she changed the subject and told me about the country house-parties which her parents frequently attend. Her mother takes three trunks full of clothes.

'Just for three days?' I asked.

'Of course. She could never wear the same thing twice. In the morning she must change from, for instance, a walking or riding ensemble into something suitable for lunch. Then she wears an afternoon dress and later a tea gown, and finally, of course, an evening gown.'

'What are her dresses like?'

'Oh Helen, she has so many.'

'Describe your favourite.'

'My favourite is pink and has a very low-cut bodice.' She pointed to the middle of her chest.

'No.'

'Yes, and it makes her waist look as small as this.' She put her middle fingers and thumbs together to make a circle.

'When your mother is not getting dressed, what does she do?'

'Sometimes she plays croquet or tennis. Mama is an expert tennis player. But of course it's the meals that take up the time.'

'Why?'

'Well, it takes your family an hour to eat two courses. Imagine how long eight would take.'

I cannot imagine a meal with eight courses. How could anyone eat that much?

'And they drink different wine with nearly every course. And then they dance or play cards.'

'We play cards, sometimes,' I said.

'For money?'

I don't think she likes being interrupted. She suddenly gave me a very odd sideways look. 'And then of course there's love.'

'What do you mean?'

'Well for instance, Mama's bedroom is always near Sir Richard Welsh's room.'

'Why?'

She gave me that odd look again, as if to see whether or not I would be shocked.

'Sir Richard is in love with my mother. He dances with her whenever he can. And hostesses always put their rooms next to each other.'

'What about your father, doesn't he mind?'

'Oh no. He encourages it. He likes Mama to have titled friends. He and Mama give parties too, at Chelney. Nicholas and I are allowed to appear at them sometimes. I love that.'

'And what do you do while your parents are away at the weekend?'

'I stay in London with the servants. I have a companion called Miss Pinner.'

'I should miss Mother dreadfully if she went away like that.'

'Oh, one gets used to it.'

I should never like it. Mother went away once for a week after she had been ill. I hated it. The house was very lonely. Father was out such a lot on calls and Mrs Bubb in a very bad temper.

'Why is your father so rich?' I asked. I hope it wasn't a rude question.

'He's a financier. His job is to do with money and business. He's getting richer all the time and wants to mix with the best people to improve our social standing. You see it's difficult to be accepted in the very best houses if you're not from a good family. Of course, it's marvellous for me. By the time I come out, I shall have access to

61

all the best circles. Father hopes I shall make a brilliant marriage.'

I think of Roundstones with its smooth white walls and black painted window frames. It's quite small, I suppose, but so comfortable. My father is sometimes abrupt in his manner but he loves Mother and me. He looks after the Makepeace family and others like them even when they can't pay him. That's what's important to him. And although Mother only has five or six dresses she doesn't mind. She likes cooking and visiting. She is very happy. And I can't imagine her having a lover. What an extraordinary thing. My uncle seems to accept this Sir Richard Welsh – he actually encourages his wife. Perhaps he doesn't love Aunt Suzanna as much as my father loves Mother.

Sophia has told me so much about her family – so much that is private. She has honoured me by confiding in me. Someday, when I have the courage, and am sure of her, I shall return these confidences.

In the meantime, I must find ways to stop her getting homesick. She often looks very sad. I know that I am not very good company. Mother tells me that I'm a terrible dreamer and sometimes seem to be in my own world. I must try harder to entertain my cousin. I hope she knows how much I care for her.

SATURDAY, 24 JULY 1909

I've made up my mind. Tomorrow I shall talk to Sophia about my people. She keeps telling me things, giving me books, sharing her feelings with me. I feel so dull some-times, unable to contribute anything of interest to our conversations. I must repay her with something. I hope she will understand. Will she laugh at me? A little at first perhaps, but not when she has been to the Tunnel Woods.

I am afraid that once she has left Needlewick she will forget me, and I shall lose her. It is so lovely to have a real companion. I am very jealous when she talks to me about Nicholas. I feel shut out from their relationship which is silly of me. How could I have expected to be a part of their lives before now? I'd love to have had a brother. It's the little things she says that make me long to be part of how my two cousins are together. 'We write notes to each other in code,' she says, 'symbols instead of letters, so if they were found nobody else would understand them.' Or, 'Nicholas is very wicked sometimes – makes up stories about those friends of our parents we don't like because they patronise or ignore us. My favourite is: "The Adventures of Lord Binky" (not his real name). In Nicholas's stories Lord Binky is so mean he makes his wife sleep on a bed of newspapers in an outhouse.'

Sophia misses Nicholas very much. I want her to stop thinking about him so she can concentrate on me. If I show her my people she will know that I too have someone special to love, and perhaps she will love me all the more because she'll be trying to make me love my people less.

I cannot wait to see her face when I tell her about them. I have kept my knowledge of them to myself for so long. And of course, once I have told her, I shall be able to visit them again. I have missed them during the past week, but I have never really been able to get away.

Sophia would think it strange if I left her alone for a whole afternoon.

So I am determined. Tomorrow, after lunch, I shall take her to the river and we'll lie on the smooth ground under the willow, and I'll tell her. I am very nervous and excited. If she laughs at me I shall be very hurt, for myself and for the sake of my people who are so easily offended. And I know they have always warned me against telling my secret to anyone, but that was before I knew Sophia. I'm sure when they meet her they will understand.

Besides, Sophia is very worried at the moment and needs a distraction. Apart from missing her home she is very concerned about her mama. Nicholas has written at last and says his mother is very unhappy.

It seems that Sir Richard has quarrelled with Aunt Suzanna. I think that this can only be a good thing, surely. It can hardly be right for a married woman to have a lover. In my imagination, Aunt Suzanna wears one of those beautiful low-cut gowns and a swansdown boa that Sophia has often told me about, and stands before Sir Richard, who is tall and dark and wears a black evening suit. He refuses to kiss her so Aunt Suzanna turns away her head to hide her tears.

But how could Sophia's papa allow them to have become such close friends? Sophia doesn't say much about her father except that he is quiet and busy and rarely talks to her. Well my father is very busy but he always has time for me. He sits me on his knee in the leather chair by the study fire, even though mother says that I should behave more like a grown-up girl. I love him to tell me about his patients. Sophia's papa sounds frightening. I think he must be a lonely man who would actually like to be his wife's lover himself. Can social position really be so important to him that he'd allow his wife to have a love affair?

I know Sophia is very unhappy about her mama and thinks about her all the time. I say perhaps soon Aunt Suzanna will be happy with Uncle Simon again but Sophia says this is impossible because they don't love each other.

Apart from Sophia's unhappiness, which I would dearly like to help, it has been a good week because I love Sophia so much.

She makes me laugh almost hysterically at times. She says Aunt Suzanna and her friends have their own way of speaking and Sophia often uses it without thinking. 'Helen!' she cries. 'Don't you think this dress absolutely deevy?' This means 'divine'.

She was talking about a delicate lawn dress she wore to the garden party this afternoon, trimmed with yards of creamy lace and decorated in tiny brown and yellow flowers.

She and I walked ahead of my parents down the meadow to the footbridge and up the path to Middlecote Hall. Sophia seemed much happier this afternoon. She is always more cheerful when she is looking her best in one of her lovely dresses. I asked her to tell me some more funny words and she pranced along, quite undignified for her, exclaiming: 'Oh Helen, I do think your black shoes are delicatissimo. And don't you think that crop of buttercups is quite superbare?'

I tried to join in but somehow the words sounded ridiculous on my lips.

'No, no, Helen, carissimo!' shrieked Sophia. 'Not like that. You have to trill the wordares lightly. How long will it take us to reach the gardenare?'

It doesn't seem funny at all now but we laughed so much then that Mother kept asking us to share the joke.

All the stalls were spread out behind Middlecote Hall on the lawn which leads to the little bank and then the rougher ground beyond, where the daffodils grow in the spring. From a distance we could hear music and voices. The lawn, with all those figures followed by their squat shadows looked brilliantly green and lit. Bunting had been tied to each stall and from tree to tree. The big white marquee for the tea billowed and flapped. The Middlecote Hall garden party is the same every year and I always love it. It means summer, the sound of voices in the open air, summer clothes, summer flowers, the brass band and the smell of trodden grass.

Sophia was so excited. She gave everyone she met a beautiful smile. She spoke to all the Makepeace children, bought all six of them toffee apples, and was extra nice to Mrs Gresham. 'How lovely to see you!' she cried. 'You're looking absolutely wonderful, Mrs Gresham.' It seemed natural for Sophia to be addressing Mrs Gresham as one adult to another. I wish I could adopt that breezy way of talking to people which seems to come naturally to Sophia. Mrs Gresham, I've noticed, is quite distant towards Sophia. She did look lovely – Sophia was right. Apart from Aunt Suzanna in her wedding photograph, Mrs Gresham is easily the most beautiful lady I know.

She has a very small waist, a straight back and serious, dark eyes, although sometimes they have very deep shadows under them because everyone knows that Mrs Gresham has trouble sleeping.

We spoke for a while to Sir George Middlecote. He teased us by saying we should not be talking to an old chap like him when there were so many young men longing to catch a glimpse of us.

The garden party was altogether a great success even though the sun shone very hot and the tea tent was like an oven. But I love the hot smell of canvas and damp grass and the way everyone drifts around sipping at cups of tea. The women wore their best hats. Sophia says many of them are out of date but she agreed that for Needlewick they all looked very smart.

I won a coconut. I don't like coconuts so I gave it to Mrs Bubb. Mother bought a crocheted mat for the hall stand. She suggested Sophia might like to buy one for Aunt Suzanna but Sophia said her mother had hundreds of little mats and anyway such fancy items were not entirely fashionable. I believe Mrs Granger who was running the stall was rather upset. She possibly doesn't realise that Sophia moves in truly fashionable London circles.

Towards the end of the afternoon, Sir George made a speech that I could not always follow. I heard Father whisper that George had been in the beer tent far too long. Usually I am asked to pick out winners of the draw but this year Sophia volunteered and everyone clapped as she presented the prizes.

Our Michael won some scent. He is an odd boy and lay in wait for us on the way home. Mother and Father were walking ahead and he suddenly appeared beside Sophia and held out the bottle.

'You can have it,' he said.

'Oh, thank you!' she said. Then she undid the top and sniffed. 'Cheap rubbish,' she murmured to me. It did smell rather over-sweet but I hope Michael didn't hear. He wouldn't understand that she is used to expensive perfume. He has never given me anything.

I'm tired. These gatherings always wear me out and the sun made my head ache by the end. Sophia was also tired by this evening and has been quiet since supper.

I feel so pent-up about tomorrow, I scarcely know how I shall get through the time until after lunch when we will be under the willow and I shall be telling her my secret.

WEDNESDAY, 28 JULY 1909

My people are angry with me. They say I should never have told Sophia – she will laugh at me and destroy the friendship I have with them. They tell me I am a fool. They say it is vanity that made me tell Sophia about them – I needed to boast, to prove I was special.

I am so sad I can scarcely move my pen. I am crippled by sadness. What have I done? I feel innocent of vanity. I only wanted to share with Sophia because I love her and she has confided so much in me.

I wish Sophia had not come to Needlewick. I do love her but I blame her for my people's anger. But that's wrong of me. If it is anyone's fault it is mine for misunderstanding things, or theirs for not listening to me.

Today was a sky blue pink day. I lay in my bed and

watched a brilliant strip of sunlight pierce the gap between the curtains. I wish I could return to this morning and be happy again.

I thought I was doing right. Sophia is different from anyone else – she is my cousin and in the past couple of weeks has become like a sister to me. I trust her. How could I keep this huge secret from her?

But my people are strange. I pretend to myself that they love me but I don't think they know what love is, at least not our kind of love.

Anyway, Sophia and I sat under the willow, exactly as I'd planned, and I told her. She was hardly listening at first, because she was still thinking about a letter she'd received from her brother yesterday. I thought it was the right time to talk about my people, because it would give her something else to think about, but I was wrong.

The words didn't come out right at all. 'There is something I've been meaning to confide in you, Sophia. A secret.'

'Oh good,' she said in that false voice of hers, 'I love secrets.'

'But this is a real secret and you must promise never to give it away to anyone else.'

'Ooooh of course not. Cross my heart and hope to die.'

'Well then. You see the thing is, I'm not quite like other girls.'

'Of course you're not, darling Helen, anyone can see that.'

'What I mean is, I can see things other people can't.'

'What things? Do you mean ghosts?' All this time her

69

eyes were shut and she was saying things she didn't really mean.

'Not ghosts, no. People.'

'What people?' She was a bit irritated, I could tell, because I was taking so long.

'I can't give them a name. I go to the Tunnel Woods and they meet me there. They are from another world.'

Now she was wide awake at last. 'What *are* you talking about?'

'I'll show them to you if you like.'

At first Sophia seemed excited about going to the Tunnel Woods. It was very breezy. The wind kept lifting her hair from her shoulders and the cow parsley along the meadow path made her sneeze. Everything rippled and swayed in expectation. The fresh green of the birch trees along the stream rustled and made me feel even more gloriously happy. Sophia laughed at me for racing ahead and then running back to her so that she would not be left behind.

She was tired by the time we reached the Tunnel Woods. I suppose it is a long walk but she made it worse by wandering along so slowly. I almost became irritated with her. I am so used to that path now I never think about distance. And it's so lovely in the valley. On one side is the stream which is clear and lively at the moment because of all the rain we had before Sophia came. At some points there are wide stepping stones. I danced about on these, hopping from one to another, trying to make Sophia join me but she was afraid of splashing her dress. To the left of the river there is first a thin coppice and then the trees disappear and there are open fields and the path is slightly banked up beside the stream to prevent flooding. The meadows are full of flowers at this time of year, buttercups and tansy. Then, when the path plunges into a copse there is a hint of how the shadows will be in the Tunnel Woods. After that there is a stretch of ripening corn and then, at last, the Tunnel Woods.

I was so excited that I wanted to carry straight on until I reached my people but Sophia said she was tired and hungry and needed to regain her strength before we entered the woods. So we sat by the stream and ate our tea and I stripped off my stockings and dabbled my hot toes. The water was so cold it made my feet ache. Sophia said my ankles would turn brown if I exposed them to sunlight. I suppose they are a little brown already but nobody sees them except me and I love the feeling of grass and stream water on them.

Sophia was miserable. She nibbled at her bread and jam and kept swatting impatiently at flies, although I warned her this is not the way to deal with them. They were a great nuisance today – they seemed to come from miles around to buzz about us as we ate our picnic. I was not bitten but Sophia seemed to be particularly attractive to them and her skin came up in great bumps. They even bit her behind her ears. She seemed so tired and annoyed I suggested that perhaps we should visit my people some other time – I wanted them to meet her when she was in a good mood. But she said: 'I've come so far; I might as well not give up now.'

I said, 'I'm sorry, Sophia, for bringing you so far.'

She smiled at me. 'Nonsense, the heat has given me a headache, that's all.'

As we entered the Tunnel Woods, I felt the cool shade cloak me in soft, dappled browns. The wood was quiet and sleepy in the afternoon sun and smelt sweet. The nettles along the path grow very strong because no-one ever goes that way except me. They seemed to be even thicker today. I suppose, because I was worried about Sophia, the path appeared to be full of obstacles. She kept brushing her hands against the stinging nettles. I found her a dock-leaf but she threw it away.

At last we began to climb away from the brook. The path there is steep but I usually enjoy that part of the journey so much because there are surprises along the way. Suddenly there's a tiny clearing where the sun throbs warm on lush grass or I come across a little pool of dark water with flies skipping over its surface. Or I might notice especially the bulging trunk of an oak tree or a bank of dead leaves. And all the time I grow more excited because I know I am nearly with my people. And so I usually love climbing up the muddy path, criss-crossed by roots which act as steps, each step taking me nearer. But every time we came to a particularly steep part today, I thought of Sophia and how tired she already was. She was perspiring a good deal. Her face was wet.

At the tunnels she stopped. 'I can't go in there,' she whispered.

'Why not?'

'It's so dark; I can't see the end.'

I had never thought of the tunnels as frightening, even

on the day I first found them. 'Don't worry,' I told her. 'Hold my hand.'

She tugged against me all the way along and her nails dug into my palm. I had to pull her up the pile of rubble between the two sections of tunnel because she was afraid of falling.

'It's not far at all now,' I said. 'This is the exciting bit, where the bracken grows above your head.'

But she said she didn't like bracken because it smells so sour. I could hear her kicking at stalks as she trudged behind me. Even in the bracken it was very hot.

In the clearing the breeze stirred the soft tufty grass and the leaves of the surrounding trees. The air was sweet and woody. I had no sense that my people were there. We wandered all round. At last I made Sophia sit at the edge of the clearing and I went to the hawthorn. I laid my cheek against its rough bark and waited.

Sophia sat very still. I could feel her watching me intently. Suddenly I felt foolish. How odd she must have thought me. She must have wondered at me leaning there against the hawthorn tree. But I still waited, even though I've never had quite that feeling of shame and awkwardness before. It was cool in the shade of the hawthorn tree with the wind ruffling the branches. Finally I forgot all about Sophia. In my hands were dry leaves, crisp and warmed by the sun.

There was anger.

Such anger.

It burned my lips and cheeks and thrust my head back against the tree. I was dazed by their anger.

I said: 'I've brought my cousin.'

But only their rage replied, tearing at the grasses and the blue sky.

How, how had I done wrong? How had I betrayed them? Every blade of grass stood on its own, separate, and the clearing was silent. I had been chosen. And I had been chosen because I was alone.

But now I have someone and she is precious to me. When I touch her hand I feel her warm skin. Her hair is silk and she lets me comb it. She is full of life and knowledge. She gives and gives for no reason but that she loves me. I have nothing to give in return but the clearing. Isn't it mine to give?

Laughter then, but not kind.

Sophia was standing beside me, her face white, her eyes fixed on my face.

I was crying.

She took my hand. 'What happened?' she asked.

'You saw what happened.'

'Saw? I saw nothing. Only you.'

'Yes, they're gone now.'

'But Helen, who are gone?'

'My people.'

'Oh Helen, you don't need to pretend to me. I understand. But don't pretend.'

I stared at her. 'They were here, Sophia.' Then I saw the look on her face. 'You don't believe me at all, do you?'

She smiled. 'Look, I'm awfully tired. Can't we go home?'

'Yes, we'll go the quick way they showed me.'

I walked to where I thought the short-cut path wound away through the trees. But I grew anxious when I realised I couldn't find it. Surely it hadn't grown over in the two weeks since I'd last been there?

'Now what are you doing?' Sophia demanded.

'I'm looking for the path, it's a quicker way back along the top of the valley.'

But I could find no path out of the clearing except the one which led back through the tunnels. The sun was blazing down on us still. I was drained of energy.

'Oh for heaven's sake, Helen, do pull yourself together. The other path must be here if you've used it before.'

But we could not find that path. We had no choice but to trail home by the stream, almost in silence. Sophia wouldn't answer if I said something and soon I felt too miserable to speak.

When we at last arrived home, she ran straight up to her room and slammed the door. I went and lay down on my bed. I feel a little better now I have written all this down, but only a little. What should I do? I can't sleep. I keep thinking of Sophia's sulky face, of the tunnels and the hawthorn tree which gave no protection.

There is one more thing. Nicholas's letter. I feel sick about that too. Usually Sophia reads her letters by herself and then finds me and tells me all about what's been happening in London. But yesterday she took her letter away and didn't come back. Eventually I went to find her.

'Are you all right?' I asked. I sat beside her and took her hand, which felt cold.

'How can I tell you,' she said, 'after all the things I've said? How can I tell you how unhappy everything is?'

'What do you mean?'

She was silent for a long time. Then she gave a deep

sigh. 'You won't understand but I'll tell you anyway. I have been lying to you. What do you know about my papa?'

'I know he's very rich. I do not understand him.' I was thinking of how he had allowed his wife to become so friendly with another man.

'Papa is a terrible man. He's cold. I hate him. He's cold and cruel. He laughs at me and Mama. He gives her presents of jewels, money, gowns, and then laughs at her for enjoying them. He goes to parties and to country houses and all the time he sneers. How could I expect you to understand? You live in such a cosy little world. Your parents love each other. My papa just uses my mother. It's not enough for him to be rich, he wants to be accepted, so he uses her loveliness to get invited to houses where he wouldn't otherwise be asked.'

I have seen a wedding photograph of Uncle Simon and Aunt Suzanna. She is very small and slender. Her hair is fair and tumbles softly over her forehead. Her eyes are large, her nose narrow and delicate. She has a little crease on either side of her mouth, as if made by smiling.

My uncle is tall and thin. His gazes straight ahead. He rests his hand on my aunt's shoulder.

'So what has happened now?' I whispered.

Apparently there has been a dreadful argument. Nicholas overheard it. He was in the library and they didn't know he was there. My uncle was in the drawing room, ready to go to a reception. Aunt Suzanna came in, still wearing her afternoon gown. She said she wouldn't go anywhere else with my uncle or with Sir Richard. She said they both used her and did not care for her at all – they just wanted somebody pretty to be seen with so they could be envied by other men. They treated her as a toy to be picked up and played with when they chose. She knew that Uncle Simon only allowed her to be with Sir Richard because he was titled and would help them get invited to great houses. She has quarrelled with Sir Richard too – she realised that he only wanted her because she was a famous beauty.

My uncle was very angry. He listed all he had done for her in the past, how much she had cost him. He commanded her to go out with him and when she refused he strode over, seized her shoulders, and began hitting her across the neck and face. Nicholas shouted out. Since then my uncle and aunt have not spoken to each other. Nicholas talks only to his mother, who will see no-one but him.

When Sophia told me all this I started to shiver. I believe I cried out when she said how her mother had been beaten. I have seen a drunkard in the village strike his wife. I cannot imagine someone like my uncle hitting a woman.

Sophia says I mustn't tell anyone about this. Her mother told Nicholas he mustn't write to her about it but he felt he had to, because it's too important a secret to keep from her.

Sometimes life is so sad. I was so much happier when I started writing this diary. Now I don't even feel sure of my people. And I keep worrying about Aunt Suzanna. He might hit her again.

SUNDAY, 1 AUGUST 1909

I feel so much better than when I last wrote. I have seen my people again. And yesterday we all went on a marvellous picnic; the Greshams, the Middlecotes and our family, even Father. The weather was not particularly kind but we had such fun.

I went by myself to visit my people on Friday and I had a delicious walk to the Tunnel Woods. A strong breeze blew. Warm air swept about my face and legs – I felt beautiful as I dashed along the path. The sunlight shone on the river. I love staring up into the great trees and seeing a blue gleam between the leaves. And I love the solid brownness of the tree trunks.

Even so I did not feel quite as carefree as I usually do when I go to the clearing. I was anxious about what would happen there.

It is odd. On Friday the tunnels frightened me. I have never been afraid of them before. But they seemed so dark and long, and I kept remembering Sophia's fear of them. But eventually I came through safely and hurried to the clearing. There was no one about. I sat on the soft grass and gazed up at the sky. Tiny clouds raced above the clearing. Everything was heavy and rustling. The sun was warm on my face.

Of course they came.

The leaves whispered, the hawthorn stirred and the grasses were bright in the sunlight. All around the woods were great with wind. I thought they had changed but they said it was I who had changed.

My eyes, they said, had grown old.

How can eyes grow old?

There was no reply.

Next time, shall I bring Sophia?

Bring her, bring her, what does it matter?

Will she see you, will she?

Bring her, bring her.

They came, and the breeze was soft on my cheeks. Lovely breeze and soft, singing leaves.

When it was time to leave I found the other way out of the woods with no difficulty.

As I walked home I did feel better. I have not lost them. I found the other path. I will bring Sophia again and then she'll see. Oh, is it greedy to want both her and them? I don't think so.

I trod so easily, as if walking were no effort at all. I looked across the valley and loved Middlecote Hall with its square, large-windowed walls all honey-coloured, in the afternoon sunshine. I waved at the tiny figure of a man in the field above. He stood with his shadow stretched out clearer than himself. He did not see me. I do not know who it was.

I love the old elms I pass on my way home by the short-cut path they showed me. They stand in a group of three on the edge of a field, bending slightly together, huge and graceful and very strong, their roots banking up the soil. When I look at the elm trees everything is firm and pure and everlasting.

The picnic was yesterday. Unfortunately the weather had broken and it was a grey, damp day and the wind blew more strongly than ever. It was a wild day.

The Greshams bicycled to Stonyfort Hill. The rest of

us drove. Sophia wore a sprigged dress with a broad sash. I wondered if she'd be warm enough. Mother had made me wear my brown wool dress though the sleeves are too tight. She said we would be very chilly and exposed on the hill.

The wind whipped and tore at the hedgerows and blew up dust in the lane. Father was in good spirits and talked to the horses in such a comical way I couldn't stop giggling.

The picnic was hilarious. The Greshams had arrived first and Mrs Gresham had a table-cloth wrapped round her – she kept trying to lay it flat against the wind. She made my mother and Lady M, Sophia and me each sit on a corner until it was weighed down by food. We all said how ridiculous it was to have a picnic in such weather. Sophia was cold so Father wrapped her in the huge plaid blanket from the trap and said she looked like a Red Indian squaw with her dark hair and skin and the blanket.

She sat huddled up while Mrs Gresham asked after her mother. I felt dreadfully sorry for Sophia but she said: 'Oh Mama is wonderfully well. I hear from her and my brother regularly. We are such a close-knit little family, you know.'

She is so brave, covering her sadness like that. Mrs Gresham said, a little coolly, and almost as if she were laughing at Sophia: 'How very fortunate for you all.'

Sophia said dreamily: 'I miss them all dreadfully.'

'I expect you do,' said Lady Middlecote sympathetically, 'but at least here you have Helen, who must be like a sister to you.'

'Yes,' Sophia replied, 'what more could I ask? I have Helen.'

There was something in the way she spoke which made me feel terribly unhappy suddenly.

I think Mrs Gresham must have noticed because she got up and asked me if I'd like a go on her bicycle.

I seemed to ache from being so long on the grass. But riding the bicycle was so exciting. I've done it quite often before and I always feel terrified at first. Then Mr Gresham took hold of the cycle and I felt much safer. He ran down the track beside me with his hand on the saddle and I loved the sense of speed and the wind on my face and hair.

Poor Mr Gresham was soon red and panting. We staggered back up the hill with the bicycle between us. At the top he rested it against a tree and put one arm round me and the other round his wife who'd been waiting there for us, leaning against the trunk with her head thrown back and her skirts flapping so that it was almost as if she had melted into the tree. When we got back to the picnic. Father and Sir George were smoking and mother and Lady M were holding on to their hats and chatting about the forthcoming wedding of Lady M's niece, Catherine. We are all invited because Mother and Mrs Gresham knew Lady Middlecote and her sister Deborah so well when they were little girls together.

Sophia was sitting apart from the others, reading a book her brother had sent her. I know it's silly but I sometimes feel a bit jealous when she is reading. She gets so involved in the story and scarcely seems aware of what's happening around her. Her current book is called

Audrey and is about a girl whose entire family is killed by an Indian tribe.

I sat next to her, thinking she might be feeling lonely. She turned to me at once and held my hand.

'Cousin Helen,' she said.

We have a great joke of calling each other 'cousin'. She has never touched me like that before. I keep looking at my hand, and remembering that moment.

'Do you mind if I sit here? Will I disturb you?' I asked.

'Of course not. You know there is no one else I'd rather be with.'

I turned my head so she would not see my tears.

THURSDAY, 5 AUGUST 1909
It has been so hot this week I have not felt like writing. It's difficult to sleep. However, although we have been complaining about the heat, we hope the weather will hold for Saturday. I am so excited. I've only been to one other wedding before, when I was four so I can scarcely remember it. Sophia says she has been to several, so I expect this country wedding won't seem very grand to her. It is lovely to have Sophia here to share the excitement.

Mother has been refurbishing my best primrose dress. She has added lace ruffles to the neck and hem, and Lady Middlecote has given me some scraps of white swansdown which is fearfully expensive. I thought the result was quite beautiful. Sophia said: 'Yes, it's lovely but when you come to choose your own dresses I suggest strong colours and much plainer styles. But of course that's *magnifico* – so summery and ideal for a wedding.'

She has a white dress with a chiffon overskirt and the

most dainty green embroidery. I told her she looked like a Kate Greenaway picture and she said: 'Good heavens, I'm not pretty in the least.'

'No,' I said and then added very softly: 'no Sophia, you are not pretty, you are beautiful.'

She smoothed her hair which always hangs in a shining mass straight across her back and looked pleased. 'Ah, if you could see my mother and her friends you would not say that.'

My mother has a delightful new hat in pink and blue.

I'm longing to see the bride and her dress. Sophia has pattern books and magazines and a Harrods catalogue her brother sent her and we spend hours browsing through them. She says the only person in Needlewick who is truly elegantly dressed is Mrs Gresham. I didn't mention that Mrs Gresham makes most of her own clothes.

We went to tea with Mrs Gresham but I don't think Sophia liked it there much. I love the garden; there is a high wall all round and a little gate leads under an arch and on to a flagged path up to the front door. The whole garden is full of mysteries. Little higgledy-piggledy paths divide the garden into shrubbery, kitchen garden and a sweet hedged area full of roses and with a little pond where Mrs Gresham has her special place. We sat in this part of the garden under a tree and sipped tea. Sophia says she does not like sitting under trees because you never know what might fall on your head.

The trouble is that Mrs Gresham always asks after Aunt Suzanna. Poor Sophia has to be so reserved – it must be a strain answering these questions.

Yesterday Mrs Gresham began, 'How is your mother, Sophia?'

'She's very well.'

'You always say that. I wish you could give me more news of her. She hasn't written to me for many months now. She and I used to be so close.'

Sophia said, 'I don't hear from her very often myself at the moment.'

'Your brother writes frequently though, doesn't he, Sophia? He's so much better now,' I said, trying to change the subject.

'Oh yes. He keeps me in touch.'

'I expect your mother is too busy going to parties to spend much time writing to you, Sophia,' Mrs Gresham said. Her voice sounded unusually harsh.

Sophia became a little angry. She loves her mother so much. 'My mother has not been to a party for a fortnight as far as I know. She's been going to meetings. She is a very serious person.'

I wondered what she meant. The last Sophia had told me about her mama was that she was keeping to her room and was desperately unhappy.

'What kind of meetings?'

'With other women,' said Sophia, toying with a crumb of bread and butter.

Mrs Gresham was sitting with her hands folded in her lap, her fair head slightly on one side. She looked quite young with the sunlight behind her. 'I must write to Suzanna,' she said softly. Then we helped to clear the tea and talked about other things.

I can't think for long about anything except the

wedding. And tomorrow I'm going to take Sophia to the clearing again. I do hope they will be kind to her. Oh my life is so good and full.

SUNDAY, 8 AUGUST 1909

The last few days have been so dreadful. Is it always the case that something you've really looked forward to will be a disappointment? Sophia says it is best never to look forward to anything and then nice things can only be a pleasant surprise.

I took her to see my people on Friday. I cannot think of them at the moment except with distaste. Cruel games, they play. They hate Sophia.

And then on the way home it was so hot I was dizzy and faint. And all the way I felt as if we were being followed, which is stupid because I know no-one goes to those woods except me, and certainly no-one else knows the other way home. And Sophia irritated me because she kept asking me questions. She does not understand at all.

And yesterday the wedding, instead of being the joyful event I had expected, was awful. Either the heat or the motion of the carriage unsettled me but I felt quite ill. My head was heavy and hot. I hardly dared eat all day because of the journey home.

A terrible storm blew up. I felt so afraid – I don't know Hippingdean at all and it seemed so dark there. The church was oppressively dim. I could not concentrate on the service. I have a vague memory of a misty white gown, of the bridesmaids in lavender and of the organ crashing. I felt cold and a hot rushing feeling kept coming to my head. I wished I was back at Roundstones in the kitchen with Mrs Bubb. The kitchen is always so comforting on bad days.

I was lonely at the reception and quite unable to eat. Sophia was busy talking to some friends. It was nice to see her meet people she knew. I believe she must have missed her London acquaintances so much since she's been at Roundstones. Mother, of course, talked mostly with Lady Middlecote and her sister Deborah Parditer, mother of the bride, and they discussed the other guests and the wedding or greeted old friends and that was odd too because for the first time in my life I felt jealous of mother because she has these friends whom she has known forever and who share everything. I thought Sophia and I might be like that but she doesn't seem to need me at all. Father was with the men so I sat on my own most of the time on a hard stool. It is so unlike me to feel unhappy and out of sorts in such a gathering. Usually I love to watch everyone and to hold my secret about my own friends, my people, very close. Then later I can tell them all about it.

But on Saturday I felt as if a pane of glass was between me and the other guests. I could see them but could not reach them. I saw the laughing, talking, eating mouths, the full, colourful skirts of the ladies, the black, sober legs of the men, the clutter of furniture and the expensive red and blue flowered carpet, the great dining-room table covered with presents, silver candlesticks, huge tureens, dainty figurines, but all the time the boom of the storm was in my ears. And when I reached inside my head for my people as I usually do when I feel lonely I could not find them, or properly remember them. I was so pleased when Mother at last told me it was time to leave and yet, as we prepared to go, I felt upset, as if I had lost something very important.

Sophia kissed lots of people goodbye and seemed bright and glowing. She has mixed with so many people in her life and attended so many grand functions. I wish I had more experience of the world. I've been dreadfully shut away in Needlewick. Mother is the same. How can she teach me about life when she has hardly ventured beyond Needlewick herself? How unlike her sister she is. Aunt Suzanna has done and seen so much more, mostly because she married a rich man and Mother only a country doctor. Sophia says I may go and stay with her in London one day but what would I find to talk about? Anyway, Sophia's home seems such a muddle these days. I do not understand Aunt Suzanna at all. How can she give up her beautiful life to attend dreadful meetings which her husband doesn't approve of – which is what Sophia says is happening.

No, I'm afraid I would feel fearfully in the way – or 'de trop' as Sophia says – were I to go and stay with her. But then Needlewick, Roundstones in particular, seems so dull now. I sit at table and hear Father suck on his spoon as he eats soup. And Mother chatters on and on about such dull topics. Do you know Sophia has even been to a Coronation? Oh, what I would have given to have been there and seen Queen Alexandra in her bell-skirted white dress and ermine-trimmed cloak! Sophia remembers the star the Queen wore at her breast flashing in the sunlight.

Sophia has seen so much in her fourteen years. I feel as

if I have done nothing. Life for me has been wasted so far.

It is so stupid to cry. I feel such an odd mixture of worry and loneliness tonight.

There is one last thing about which I must write. I want to confess it and hope that, having written it, it will go away.

I am jealous of Sophia.

I had not realised it before but when I watched her, so beautiful with the gaslamps reflected in her hair at the reception on Saturday, surrounded by admiring people, I felt envious. She has everything, I nothing. She has beauty and charm, talks easily, has many friends, wealth, even a brother, and her family owns two great houses. And I? I have nothing. I don't even think I have Sophia's love as I once believed. I suppose other people who were at the reception on Saturday were so much more interesting than me. I know I'm dull. But I think Sophia, if she had cared for me, might have spent a little time with me when I was so lonely, sitting by myself in that crowd.

I suppose now I am suffering from self-pity. That is what Father would say, I know.

Sophia has lent me a book called *Little Lord Fauntleroy*. I must read that, perhaps it will cheer me up. She says it's a child's book but that I may enjoy it. I know that in her eyes I am no more than a child.

WEDNESDAY, 11 AUGUST 1909
Everything has gone. I shall never see my people again.

Yesterday I lay in bed, pretending to be ill, thinking

about what happened on Monday. How can my people come back? They were right to mistrust me – they will never again reveal themselves to me.

They saw Michael lying beneath the leaves, scheming to frighten and shock me. Or perhaps he was just interested to see how I would react. What hurts more than anything else is that he must have been following me for weeks to have known when and where to hide. He followed me to where I thought I could be entirely private and alone. He must have seen me with my people. I feel as if my most private being has been stripped open and spat on.

But they would understand that Michael is only a child and not quite right, and therefore not quite responsible – but Sophia, what must they have thought of her?

I am sure that she knew of Michael's scheme, probably even invented it. Why else did she come with me to the clearing, when I know she hates that long walk and doesn't believe in my people? And why did she specifically tell me to go and sit under the tree?

She knew Michael would be there.

I cannot escape the horror. I will always remember it.

Some times are like that, there is a significance and then I don't forget. There was a significance in the way I felt when I woke, the way my dress fell over my head as I put it on, the taste of the morning tea, too strong and not quite hot enough. The weather was all wrong, all wrong, cool, breezy, damp, the summer blown away and autumn come in the woods and by the river in yellowed grasses and the muddy path and the angry brown ripples on the water. Everything was damp, the air soaked though it wasn't raining, and my body was almost too heavy to walk. Fungus had grown in the roots of trees, terrible, spotted toadstools. I cried for the memory of the violets and the primroses in the spring. Come back lovely spring, before Sophia. I am crying now. See how the ink has smeared.

Sophia *knew*.

'Why are you crying?'

'No reason.' But because on the way to the woods I loved her still I said, 'I hated the wedding.'

'Why?'

'I felt so lonely.'

She laughed, of course. 'Oh Helen, you should make more effort. You can't have been lonely with all those people about.'

'It's easy for you. You're used to talking to strangers.'

'You must learn to take an interest in the other person, then you'll get on much better.'

Is that all conversation is? What kind of interest does she mean?

She shouted in the tunnels. She's always been afraid of them, she said she wanted to see if there was an echo but I know it was to deafen her fear. And to signal Michael that we were nearly there.

The clearing was empty. No one would come, I knew that. It was too damp, too much unhappiness in me. But Sophia told me to relax, they'd come if I left her at the edge of the clearing and went to the tree so I lay back against the trunk, closed my eyes and waited for the softness and the light inside.

There was a sound near my foot, a rustle. I opened my

eyes though I knew they would not come. The leaves moved. I knew it wasn't them.

I have always been so safe. I don't remember being much afraid.

There was a little white hand. Dirtied, bloodied.

And then in a rush, a great spurt of movement, Michael. A grin, a sneer, a gesture, and he was gone.

My breath caught in my lungs. Sophia was laughing. First I heard her, then I saw her. She was laughing so much there were tears on her cheeks.

And then she came and put her arms round me and her hair fell across my face as she drew me close and kissed me and made little hushing noises as if to a baby. 'Hush, ssh, Helen, hush. It's all right. It was only Michael. What a stupid trick!'

But I had seen her laughing.

I have repeated to my people so often that Sophia is loyal and trustworthy but now I have been reading the past entries in my diary and realise how little I understood. Sophia, who I have described as being my supporter and friend, stood there speechless with laughter to see me like that, crouched in the leaves so ridiculously.

I would not speak to her all the long way home.

She couldn't bear me to be quiet. She said: 'Well, never mind, it'll be all right next time.'

Then: 'Would you like me to come with you again tomorrow, Helen? I don't mind.'

And she asked again and again: 'Are you all right now? Do you feel all right?'

Later she said: 'You're far too old for this now,

anyway, Helen. You've been a lonely girl, tucked away in a small village. But now you've got me, at least. I'll introduce you to people. You can visit me in London often, as I've told you.' This was how she tried to comfort me.

So my people were right about her. They are right to despise her.

She is deceitful, how she must have laughed at me behind my back when I first revealed my secret to her. She is cruel, it is funny for her to see me, her cousin, who has poured out so much love for her, hurt and unhappy.

But quite apart from Sophia's deceit and Michael's trickery, I know their main reason for deserting me is that I have been so weak myself. In the clearing I was paralysed by fear, unable to move, stifled by the horror of those few moments. How can such a weak being expect favours?

I am left with bitter feelings of regret, and longing for Sophia's departure. After all, she is nothing but a doll dressed in expensive clothes and a tongue ready with cruel witticisms. She is frightfully bored with anything that doesn't rotate round herself. The things I most admired about her mean nothing now. Her beauty is worthless to any but herself, her experience of the world has not taught her kindness, and even her precious brother, I suspect, is as cruel and lacking in understanding as she.

Instead of delighting in her company here, I now feel that she is a great bluebottle spoiling everything she touches, and destroying my peace. I can't help blaming her for all that has happened, not just Monday's incident.

I would have enjoyed the wedding had she not been there, surrounded by admirers. She drains away the friendly feeling of the gatherings I go to with my parents and their friends, and replaces it with something uncomfortable and competitive. Even the picnic was not as happy for me as picnics usually are because she was there, isolating herself. How glorious the summer promised to be before she came.

Now autumn is almost here. All about me the green is dusty and worn out. And what have I to look forward to now, but days of endless boredom – school for a few more terms and then many dull years at home before I get married, if anyone will have me? When I had my people I was the most blessed person on earth. Now I am the most unhappy.

I am haunted by hateful memories. I remember the storm at Hippingdean, the stillness which lay over everything on that dreadful journey, as if a blanket had smothered all sound. I remember how frightened I was when I heard that rumble of thunder as we entered the church. At night I lie and think of those stained glass windows flickering with strips of lightning, and the damp smell of the women's wraps. And I remember the endless drum drum of the rain, even through all the happy noise of the reception and the dark windows so black compared to the lit rooms.

I remember that storm and how frail it made me feel. I am so aware of my own smallness suddenly. While I had my people I was someone marked out and special, but now I am precisely what I'm sure Sophia thinks I am, an ugly, unintelligent nobody. I'm not even a man. If I were

I might, just might, have got away from Needlewick some day.

It's odd, isn't it, that I don't hate Michael? He's an unlovable boy, but I can't hate him, whereas Sophia makes me almost wince with hatred when I see her now.

EVENING

After I had finished writing the above, I couldn't bear to be in the house any longer, so I walked into Needlewick. I had no idea where I was going. Sophia was reading in the garden and luckily did not press to come with me.

It is warm again. The lane was dry and the mud rough and dusty. The flowers in the hedgerows looked as if they were dying and the cows in the meadow were tossing their tails to and fro, swatting at flies. Poor things. Today they irritated me for being so accepting of their lot. I heard a skylark and that cheered me up a little. It winged up into the blue sky above the side of the valley. I was plagued by horse-flies.

Needlewick was half asleep, of course. A few of the Makepeace children came with me to the shop where it was cool and dark. I bought them some toffee.

Afterwards I wandered up the High Street. Usually I love Needlewick but today I was bored with its sameness. Nothing was happening – even if I had met someone, there would have been nothing worthwhile for us to say. Then I reached the church. I was so hot I wandered in and rested on one of the benches. I like the church, which seems to be holding a breathful of vivid memories whenever I'm in there alone. Once I am gone the church breathes out and all the people who have cried or wed or

94

been dead there will come to life and take their place in the bones of the building once more. I told Sophia about this once. She gave me a strange stare which at the time I put down to her greater maturity. Now I know she has no imagination and no soul. She can't understand the meaning of anything you can't touch or buy.

The church comforted me. I wandered up to the lectern and ran my fingers over the fierce golden eagle perched on top. My fingers left a steamy mark on the bird's back. I gazed up at the stained glass and managed to make out the story of the Wedding at Cana. I sniffed the bowls of red roses and gypsophila and looked at the polished brasses. Yes, I felt better.

And strangely, once outside in that heat again, my feet took me to Mrs Gresham's house.

Perhaps it was the garden which drew me because it is always shady and secluded there. At the moment the apple trees are covered with green bubbles of ripening apples and the lawn is a mass of daisies and clover. Mrs Gresham says it is not worth trying to preserve a lawn planted with so many trees so she allows the daisies to grow freely. She has always said I may let myself into the garden any time even when she isn't there. I suppose I half hoped she would be out, but she was sitting under a tree wearing a large white hat and a loose dress, reading.

She glanced up and smiled.

I stood quite still because I knew I was going to cry. I wanted to explain everything to her, and the fact that I was there, alone in the garden with her, made me feel very upset yet somehow released. She looked at me for a moment and then laid down the book and asked if I would like a glass of lemonade.

She fetched it for me herself and by the time she came back I had calmed down.

'I just thought I'd come and sit in the garden,' I said.

'I'm glad you felt you could.' She picked up her book again.

After I'd finished my drink I lay back on the grass. The leaves above dappled the sunlight. I stared straight up at the blue sky through the apples and the leaves, but it was too sad to lie there watching that glittering sky when I felt so dull so I turned over and buried my nose in the grass. An ant tickled across my hand. It was very quiet.

I knew that if I wanted to talk I would have to speak first. I heard Mrs Gresham turn a page.

Finally I said: 'Sophia's mother is one of those suffragettes. Are you surprised?'

She looked at me with her blue blue eyes. 'No, Suzanna was always the one with spirit.'

'How do you mean?'

'Well, as you know, we were quite a little group, your mother and Suzanna, Lady Middlecote and Deborah, and me. We even had a name for ourselves – The Needlewick Five. Suzanna was the brilliant, pretty one. We all loved her very much, not just because she was so lovely, and children love beauty, but because she was always so cheerful and eager for adventure.'

She was silent for a while. 'We all thought she would do something special. And then she met your uncle and I suppose she was dazzled by his money and charm and the chances he offered her, and of course, being Suzanna, she quickly adapted herself to her new life. It's her way to be best at anything she does. But it is her way too, that if she should be aware that something is wrong, that her life is not as fine as she had imagined and hoped, she would rush out and look for something better. She tried a lover, and now she realises perhaps that it is her marriage and her gender that are trapping her, and so she seeks to alter that situation.' Looking back, I'm surprised she knew so much about Aunt Suzanna, but then Mrs Gresham knows everything.

'Oh I should like to be free too!' I cried.

Mrs Gresham gave me an odd look. 'What can you mean, Helen?'

'I feel trapped, Mrs Gresham. What hope is there for me?'

This was not what I had intended to talk to her about when I first came to the garden. I had wanted to complain about Sophia.

'But I thought you loved Needlewick, Helen. Or has your cousin given you ambitions to go to London and become an ornament of society?'

'No, certainly not. All she wants is to be like her mama used to be. I couldn't bear that existence. Anyway, I'm not beautiful enough.'

She gave me a lovely smile. 'No, my love, I daresay you're not.'

'I used to admire Sophia but now I realise that she has no sympathy or imagination. I understand Aunt Suzanna better than Sophia does.'

Given that Mrs Gresham is not fond of Sophia, I had expected her to agree with me. Instead she sat beside me on the grass. 'Helen, don't condemn Sophia or stop loving her. You have given her so much, don't you see? You've shown her another side of life, perhaps a purer side, where people take pleasure from their family and friends and the countryside and are relatively content with these things, not always grasping after more money and possessions.'

'But I have stopped loving her. I can see straight through her. She does not care for anyone except herself.'

Mrs Gresham said: 'What has happened, Helen?'

'Nothing,' I said. But she sat waiting, in her billow of pale green skirt. 'I showed her something very secret and precious and she laughed at it and destroyed it for me.'

She was watching me closely. 'Was it so important to you that one sneer from Sophia could cause it all to blow away? And don't you think, just possibly, that Sophia may have been cruel because she was envious? You have so much – a secure home, a loving family and your independent spirit. You are a private person while Sophia is used to a surface world where no one dares look inside herself.'

'Anyway, I'll be glad when she's gone,' I said.

'I think so will I. You are not the same Helen any more.' She tugged a lock of my hair and then returned to her book.

Soon afterwards I came home.

I know that the memory of this afternoon will stay firmly in my mind for a long time to come. I smell the grass and the apples still, and hear the bees on the clover. I remember the bird droppings on the wrought iron garden table, and the porch door swung wide open, and I shan't forget any of it.

I have thought about what we said about Aunt Suzanna and Sophia. And I have considered what Mrs Gresham said about my secret. A tiny grain of hope has come. Perhaps she is right. If I care enough, I shall be able to find my people again. And oddly, creeping after this hope, comes a sense of weariness. I do not think I quite have the energy to try and find them after all. It is such a long walk to the Tunnel Woods and often they are not there and I waste my time.

Sophia has done this to me. She has drained me.

SUNDAY, 15 AUGUST 1909

I do not know where I found the courage.

Ever since Wednesday I have heard Mrs Gresham's voice asking me over and over again whether my secret is really so important if it can be destroyed so easily. At first I didn't really want to see my people again at all but yesterday morning I woke up feeling completely different. I could think of nothing but my people. I had to see them – I could not get the idea out of my mind. I'd be thinking of something different and then an image of the clearing would come.

But I couldn't visit them yesterday. First I had to go into Cheltenham with Mother and Sophia, and when I came back I noticed that Michael was in the garden. How could I be sure he wouldn't follow me? So I waited.

Evening came and of course I thought I would not be able to go to them after all, it was too late. But then at supper the feeling that I must see them was so strong that I could scarcely eat.

I made the decision to visit them during the night.

But I have always been a little frightened of the night. I gaze out of my window over the garden and the shrubs look so dark and hidden. How could I contemplate walking five miles, some of it through woodland, on my own?

But I did. I couldn't stop myself.

My parents go to bed early. By ten-thirty the house was silent. I tiptoed out without waking anyone. And as I shut the garden door I remember thinking that I had closed the door on safety and warmth and I was out in the mysterious open air of the night. It smelt so good, slightly damp and very leafy. I could smell the night itself; and I felt cheerful and strong as I plunged down the path towards the stream. There was a half moon. It was very starry. When I looked up I saw more and more stars. They dropped towards me out of the dark.

But as I neared the stream and entered the trees I felt less brave and excited and almost turned back. I began to think that my people would not be there anyway in the night. And yet I'd been so sure. Each time I thought of turning back I'd think, 'No, I'll go a little bit further.' I tried not to imagine what lay behind the trees but remembered my father's words when I once told him I was frightened of the night, 'What could be hiding in the night, Helen, that is not there in the day?' I knew that this didn't mean he would want me to be so far from home on my own, but the memory of those words comforted me.

Nevertheless, I was afraid. The night was so alive. There was a faint breeze which ruffled the leaves and sent the odd one scuffling down. The brook whispered and gurgled. I could hear it more clearly than during the day. There were rustles in the leaves, birds or animals, I suppose, and the calls of night creatures. But the stream became a symbol of safety for me. While I was beside it, I told myself, nothing could happen to me.

Being in the woods was worse. The darkness plunged about me in fits and starts. I kept twisting my feet on roots or catching them in briars. The trees stooped above me, dark shapes. I tried to recognise them as the green-leafed, shining masses they are in the day but they seemed to be holding back from me. And as I stumbled up that steep path, I suddenly remembered the tunnels. I had forgotten all about them. I wished I was back in my bed. I even wished Sophia was with me.

But I couldn't turn back. If I turned round, a host of terrible beings would be let loose from the tunnels to follow me down the path. I must not turn my back on them.

I was half sobbing when I finally reached the square mouth of that first tunnel. There was no light, none. But I had to go in because I had no choice. I could not turn my back on that blackness. I kept thinking: 'It'll be two minutes, and then you'll be out in the bracken and nearer your people. Go to them, you'll be safe. They'll look after you.' But all the time I knew that my people might not be there at all.

The dark was a physical barrier which I had to climb through. The blackness hit at my straining eyes and groped fingers through my hair. It had no mercy. It breathed on my cheeks. My feet stepped into an abyss with each stride. I kept my hand on the wall and I never knew what I'd be touching next.

I was halfway along when I thought of bats and imagined one landing on my face, wrapping its clammy wings about my eyes. I tightened my body, folded my arms and half-closed my eyes.

Until at last a dark grey light, as welcome as brilliant day to me, showed that I had come to the gap between that first tunnel and the next, and that I must climb up into the bracken.

As I fumbled up the dark slope, something clutched at my left foot, half pulling off my boot. I tried to cry out but no sound came so I kicked and ran, reached the bracken and plunged into its dark, familiar fronds and hurtled forwards. Perhaps what had held me then was ivy or some other strong, climbing plant. Perhaps my foot was caught between two rocks. I expect so.

I ran wildly, my throat hurting because my breath came in dry rasps. I ran. I ran. And stopped suddenly, amazed. For ahead of me, gleaming between the tall stems of bracken at either side of the path was light, soft, orange light. I could smell my people, that composty odour of decaying leaves they always carry with them. And then suddenly I was no longer afraid or anxious or sad.

The light came from a fire lit in the centre of the clearing, near the hawthorn tree but not scorching it. The fire-light flung the tree into a new perspective so that the branches stood out clearly, each leaf very separate, gleaming with orange light. There were no shadows within the tree, only light.

And they were there, around the fire, in the grass. And through them I could see the flames.

I sat by the fire in the warmth of flames which fingered the black night, and the dancing and the music called me. The fire was hot and bright, and the night beyond, the tunnels, were far away.

Come, leap.

I can leap through the flames, anything is possible. So I stood up and felt their transparent fingers draw me into the fire and I sprang forward, up, up over the flames. It was flying, it was becoming air. I did it again and again. Back and forth across the flames we flew, and none of us was burned. Then they let go of my hands and suddenly I knew I was leaping alone and I was afraid of being burnt.

You should never never be afraid to leap alone.

But I was afraid. I couldn't do it any more.

I felt their hands on me. It was like being in a fever, first burning hot, then cool and damp. Their hands soothed the scalding wounds. I felt them stroking and caressing. And as they touched me, they eased me away from the fire. I should have held back. I wish now I'd held back, but I didn't. It was so beautiful to be gently and soothingly brought away . . . away. Everything faded around me, as if I was fainting and the darkness was rushing through me.

After a while it came to me that I was alone at the edge of the woods. I turned back and the woods were dark behind me. They had brought me to the secret path, the quick way home. In the open fields the stars fell around me. It was good to be part of the night.

At the garden gate I hesitated but the smell of the flowers within the garden lured me in finally, although I knew that, once inside, the magic would drift away.

The roses and mignonette smelt more strongly than during the day. They were like china flowers because the garden wall sheltered them from the breeze outside.

When I was little I used to kiss the trunks of trees because I loved them, they seemed so kindly and firm. I loved their rough bark against my lips. Last night I would have done the same, but once in the garden I sensed eyes in the night and I was afraid to stay long or do anything strange. I had come back to the old world of doubts and fears.

The house felt stiflingly warm but the sheets and soft mattress of my bed were wonderful. I was worn out.

WEDNESDAY, 18 AUGUST 1909
It is Sophia's fault that I lied to her. She taught me to lie because she has been lying since her arrival – about what she really thinks of us all and about how much she cares for me. She made me lie to pay her back. And I wanted to defeat her, to send her home beaten, even if she never realises it.

She's so untouchable in her superiority that I wanted to withhold just one thing from her and she'll never know what it is. I'm loving this lie because she'll never know about it.

The other reason is her stupid camera. Ever since her brother sent it she's been showing it off. She keeps offering to let me have a go but I won't touch anything of hers, I won't owe her anything. So we've been all round the village with her Kodak because she says she must have something to remind her of lovely Needlewick. And of course, I knew it was coming, she must photograph the clearing, it's become such a special place to her she says, because of me. And she will send me a print, wouldn't I love that – to have a print of the clearing? And of course photographs can be very revealing, she says. It's well known that photographs show more then the naked eyes can see.

So on Monday we went back to the Tunnel Woods. She thought she was very grand, swinging her little Kodak on its strap, talking about the advantages of hand-held cameras and how expert her brother is at photography. And all the time I knew the clearing would be a dead place. Since Saturday night I have known that my people have gone from me for ever. Their last gift for me was their dance. I did expect there would be the charred remains of the fire and foolishly suggested as much to Sophia, wanting to show off, I suppose. I had intended to pick up some ashes as a last souvenir. But there was nothing. The clearing was absolutely bare.

I let her take some photographs of course. Why not? I sat under the tree, closed my eyes and pretended that my people were there. She might as well waste her precious film.

But on the way home I realised that this revenge was not enough. I wanted to hurt her and frighten her.

She spent yesterday in Needlewick playing the

charming heiress, handing out toffees to the Makepeace children and making them stand in a bunch outside their cottage while she took their picture. She didn't include Mrs Makepeace. I suppose she thought the children looked sweet, whereas their mother might have added a touch of hardship to the scene.

Sophia then swanked up the High Street, took a photograph of the church and arrived at the Greshams' house. Mrs Gresham didn't seem to mind posing for her. In the picture she will be standing under her favourite tree, clasping her hat, her skirts sailing out behind her in the breeze. Sophia also took a picture of Roundstones and the servants and my parents in the garden. My father stood with one hand on Michael's shoulder. Neither Michael nor Mrs Bubb was smiling; Mrs Bubb stared straight ahead at the camera, Michael looked away down to the river. I hated Sophia for taking this photograph. She will be stealing part of my home back with her.

We are having a party in her honour tomorrow night and then, at last, she will be gone.

I got my revenge. But I do not feel happy tonight as I thought I would, only disturbed and somehow dirtied because it all worked so well, she was so frightened.

We went again to the clearing.

We were very much at odds. She kept trying to win me over. By telling me how much she'd miss me and how noisy London would seem compared to Needlewick. Then she tried to gain my pity by saying that she dreaded seeing her mother again after all that had happened. I spoke as little as possible and was very sulky. But because I hated being like that and kept remembering what Mrs

Gresham had said about trying to love Sophia, several times I was near the point of taking her arm as a sign of forgiveness. But I couldn't. And I had to go on with my stupid plan. I couldn't stop myself. My will was pushing me on and I couldn't prevent it from happening.

When we came near to the tunnels on the way home I suggested we should try a game we used to play at school called 'Trust'. One person is blindfolded, the other has to direct her to do whatever she wants. If you trust the other person you will do what she says. Sophia obviously thought I was being childish but she agreed because she was determined to be kind to me. I think she quite enjoyed the game at first. I blindfolded her and led her about and called directions to her. Then we reversed positions. I stood in the dark while she told me to take three steps, turn to the left, walk backwards two steps and so on. She was good at that, she likes being obeyed. I felt the bracken around me and was very excited because of what I was going to do next.

After I had blindfolded her again I took her hand and led her down into the gap between the tunnels. She squeaked with fear as we climbed down the stony slope. Once at the bottom, I twisted her round and then led her not into our usual tunnel but to the other, far longer tunnel which she had never been in before. Then I tiptoed away. At first she called after me, laughing, but I didn't answer. Then she got annoyed and said she would take off the blindfold. But I had tied an intricate knot and wound the scarf's fringe into her hair so it took her a while to drag the blindfold off. Then she walked down the tunnel in the direction I had hoped, the wrong direction, away from the gap in the tunnels and the way home. I followed her very quietly in the dark. Once or twice I think she heard me because she stopped dead and called my name rather nervously.

At last she reached the exit and began to walk along the path which she didn't realise for a while was unfamiliar to her.

Then, when the ground began to slope upwards instead of down, she shouted, 'Helen where are you? Don't play the fool. Please! Come on!' But I stayed hidden. She was almost in tears by this time but I had my best trick to come and I wasn't going to give myself away. When she turned round and walked very fast in the direction of the tunnels I was ready for her.

I had stayed hidden near the entrance so I raced back along the tunnel and scrambled up the rubble slope which leads to the path to the clearing. Then I branched off over the top of the second tunnel until I came to the opening of the air vent I discovered last summer. My hands were full of pebbles. When I heard Sophia's footsteps below I let drop a shower of pebbles. She screamed and stopped dead. I dropped one pebble at a time. I'd allow a long pause, then, when I heard her take a step, I'd drop another. Each pebble clattered softly down the vent, making an echo of itself.

I could hear sobbing.

Eventually I ran out of pebbles. It must have been ten minutes before a rustle made me realise she was creeping along the wall of the tunnel. Seconds later she was out, racing along the path. Eventually I caught up with her beside the stream.

'Where did you get to?' I cried.

She jumped and turned to me. Her hair was untidy, her face pale and blotchy with crying and her beautiful flower-print dress stained where she had rubbed it along the side of the tunnel.

'That was cruel,' she whispered.

'What was?' I felt frightened. 'I turned round and you had gone. You must have wandered up the wrong tunnel.'

She looked at me with baffled eyes for a moment and then said: 'Oh Helen, thank heavens you're here. I was so afraid.'

I allowed her to link her hand in my arm, although I hated her even more.

I feel sad and dirty tonight. She deserved to be made unhappy but I didn't know I could be so cruel. I keep thinking of the Helen who was writing only a month ago how much she loved her cousin, and then of the excited, tight feeling at the top of my legs as I dropped the pebbles into the vent.

WEDNESDAY, 25 AUGUST 1909
Sophia has written a long, moaning, selfish letter full of lies about how she longs to be back here in Needlewick again because things are so horrible in London.

Good. I'm glad her family has broken up. I'm glad her mother has gone away.

Mother is very upset by the news and can't understand why Aunt Suzanna has left but I can. My uncle sounds a hateful man. Looking back through this diary I see that I once admired the life Sophia's mother used to lead. How wrong I was! How childish to be taken in by the fact that

Aunt Suzanna wore gorgeous clothes and went to parties. Her life must have been as empty and futile as Sophia's will be.

Mrs Gresham has been trying to make mother understand about Aunt Suzanna but of course she never will. She is so happy at home doing exactly what she likes best, endless little domestic chores and making calls. How could she understand her sister's new, violent way of life?

I cannot bring myself to write back to Sophia. I have nothing to say to her now. I can't tell her what I really think – it would be a waste because she certainly wouldn't understand. I cannot write affectionately to her, that would be a lie and I have lied enough. And if I write she will reply and I do not want to hear from her again. Her letter makes me unhappy because it is from her and I want to forget her.

Already all that happened in the clearing is gently fading from my memory. I would not dream of going back to the Tunnel Woods, because I know I'll never see my people again. But I don't feel sad, no, almost glad to be free of that secret, of knowing them and having to visit them. And that is odd because in the years I knew them I never once thought of them as being a burden. They were my dearest friends.

I wonder how long it will be before I feel happy again. I feel utterly discontented as I walk round the garden, kicking at plants, blaming Sophia for ruining everything with her boredom, her unhappy family, her scorn for all the things I used to love about my home. Now I see through her eyes what a tiny world we live in here.

Nothing happens. Some people live in Needlewick all their lives. They have no desire to see the world beyond.

But I certainly have now. I must extend my mind and thoughts. I must get away and learn what is going on. Other places are calling. Needlewick is only the beginning.

Mrs Gresham thinks I could make a career for myself if I put my mind to it. How grand that word career sounds! I have decided that my way of escape is to choose a future which will require me to go away. My father went to Cambridge and then to a hospital in London. I don't think I shall be a doctor, but I should like to study in a university. Mrs Gresham says there are scholarships to be won.

I shall tell no one about this. Mother would be amazed if she knew of my plans, and Father would think it a girlish whim. So I'll keep quiet. I shall just go ahead and do it on my own.

I have learnt to keep my secrets close.

8

May 1920

By the time she laid aside the diary Sophia was cramped and chilled and the light was fading. The willow cast a long shadow over her face and neck which were wet with tears.

She stood, went to the river and gazed along its bank in the direction of the Tunnel Woods. She had forgotten so much. The river flowed in dark ripples – she had to restrain her hand from releasing the notebooks to the water. After all, the river would not carry away her remorse. She had anticipated such a nostalgic afternoon by the willow, indulging in a package of memories provoked by the reading of Helen's diary. She could remember thinking, whilst in Needlewick that first time, what a favour she was doing Helen by keeping her company and telling her about the sophisticated world beyond. Even when Nicholas's letter brought news of her mother's flight a part of her had refused to acknowledge either his pain or her mother's suffering. Instead she had been absorbed by her own glamour; beautiful rich girl abandoned by a selfish mother. She had expected, as she began reading the diary, to smile fondly at her childish follies and then leave behind at last the Needlewick ghosts which had quietly pursued her down the years. Instead she was weeping with fear of the ghosts crowding insistently about her. Helen loved you, they said, and you destroyed her love. She gave you all she had and you pushed it away. Your mother was far away, calling for help, but you ignored her. Nicholas, who had endured her parents' break up at first hand, was treated through your letters to a showy parade of arrogant drivel.

Mrs Gresham, how could you be so cruel as to confront me with all this?

She became conscious of the night – of small noises in the reeds and grasses. If only Colin were here, she thought, he'd look after me and comfort me. But Colin was far away, she had not wanted him to come to Needlewick.

Her feet were wet with dew when she reached the house. She let herself in by the kitchen door, hoping not to attract attention, but Mrs Bubb was standing there, as if waiting for her.

'I've kept your supper warm,' was all she said, unsmiling as ever, but for the first time Sophia detected a little warmth in the bulbous grey eyes, as well as a kind of yearning.

Sophia crept up to her room, washed her face and went down to the drawing-room.

Her aunt leapt to her feet. 'Sophia! Where have you been, dear? You've missed supper. Of course it doesn't matter, we've kept you some. Oh, you look so pale!' She did not draw attention to Sophia's eyes which were red and dazzled.

'I went for a walk, further than I intended.'

'You should have waited for me. It's so lonely on your own. I was saying so to Jane this afternoon.'

The doctor, in a rare display of consideration, interrupted with an offer of brandy.

'Yes, a small glass of brandy would be very welcome. And if you don't mind I'll take it up to my room. I feel so tired.'

'Of course, and I'll bring up your supper,' her aunt said. 'We must look after you or what will your father think of us? Would you like some hot milk too?'

'No, really, thank you, aunt, and I'll collect my supper from the kitchen.' Sophia stooped to kiss her. 'Good night. Thank you.'

Her aunt was easy to please. All she asked was a little affection. Sophia hated herself for buying a glow of happiness so cheaply, with one kiss.

9

Mrs Parditer did not approve of Needlewick's new vicar who was young, unmarried, radical theologically and, according to his housekeeper, drank rather heavily. She therefore felt no compunction at not listening to his sermon on the Beatitudes and instead paid attention to his flock. The Middlecote pew, set at right angles and elevated from the rest, commanded a good view of the nave. In particular she could see the Callwoods: Harry, with the dreamy expression that signified a mental sleep; Margaret, her countenance shut up and worried; and Sophia, face shadowed by an absurdly wide hat, eyes fixed on prayer book, lips compressed. But despite the inadequacy of her view of Sophia's expression, Deborah Parditer sensed that a light had gone out in her; the confidence and youthful consciousness that had brought such vitality to the drawing-room at Roundstones had drained away.

She's seen the diary then, Deborah realised, and it has moved her, as of course it should. Deborah had read it herself during one of her vigils by Eleanor Gresham's bedside in the last weeks of her life.

Eleanor, in the final stage of her illness, had usually said little, listening instead to chapters from a favourite book, but one night she had told Deborah in her clear, deliberate voice: 'I shall bequeath Helen's diary to Sophia.'

'Which diary, Eleanor?'

'Oh, didn't you know? Helen used to keep a diary. She came to me once, years ago now, and told me that she was going to destroy it because she'd outgrown it. And I – well – even all those years ago I'm afraid I used a sick woman's privilege. I asked her if she'd let me have it.'

'And she didn't mind?'

'Not at all. I think, if anything, she was rather flattered. And I suspected she'd only told me about it in the first place because she wanted me to know about the diary. But she would not look at it again herself. She made me promise to throw it away after I'd read it.'

'Sensible girl.'

'Yes, perhaps. And in some ways I wish I'd never seen the diary. But Helen was already far different from the dreamy little girl she once was and I thought her diary would remind me of her old self. It did, but only in the pointlessly sad way that photographs reveal how time has passed and things have changed. So I only read it once. But there was one part I couldn't burn because it contained too much of Suzanna.'

After a pause during which Deborah reflected on the significance of this remark, she asked: 'Has John written to Suzanna about you, yet?'

'I won't let him write.'

'She should know about your condition.'

'I won't have her come home out of pity for me.'

'Eleanor. She would come because she is your friend.'

At last Eleanor admitted sadly: 'It does seem a long time since I heard from her.'

Deborah was seated in a low chair by the drawn curtains; Eleanor, lying against a heap of pillows, had turned her face away. The intimacy of the room was suddenly oppressive. Mention of Suzanna always seemed to have a jarring effect, there were too many conflicting feelings, too much unsaid, too many shared and unshared memories.

Eleanor murmured softly: 'You may read the diary if you like, Deborah. I'm sure Helen wouldn't mind. Read it.'

Deborah felt an instant of childish suspicion – how many times had Suzanna or Eleanor flung a book or letter at her: 'Oh, let her read it. Go on, she's dying to read it! Go on then, Deborah!' Was Eleanor mocking her now, humouring her curiosity? But no, this was being offered as a gift, Eleanor's eyes were full of affection. 'I'd like you to read it,' she said. 'I'm very tired now. It's there on the chest-of-drawers.'

When the congregation rose for the offertory, Sophia's pale face was momentarily raised to the pulpit. And now that poor girl has read it too, thought Deborah. I hope she is brash enough not to take it much to heart. It all happened so long ago and none of it was really her fault. Indeed, did not I, when faced with the same imponderable obsession, react the same way? Or would have done, had I been allowed a little closer? But Suzanna shut me out. She was much wiser than Helen and chose her confidante well.

The pain, even after all those years, was still very sharp, sharper far than that of bereavement for her husband or even for Eleanor. The pain of exclusion.

Arriving at Roundstones on a spring morning the Henshaw girls, Deborah aged fourteen and eight year old Jane, had found Mrs Bubb in the kitchen, her knuckles rubbed red and raw with the toil of washday, her face shuttered, but a triumphant flicker in her eye. 'The girls have gone out long since. They've left me to do this lot by myself.'

'Did they say where they were going, Mrs Bubb?'

'Not a word, no.'

But she knew.

Up went Deborah's chin. 'Come on, Jane, we'll call on Eleanor or go riding.'

Riding, the great salve, the Henshaw girls' way of excluding the others; only they were privileged enough as daughters of a wealthy farmer to be good horsewomen.

But just by chance they were down by the river at the end of the day to witness Suzanna and Margaret come trailing home: Suzanna first, swinging her hat, eyes aglow, step buoyant; Margaret behind, tight-lipped and exhausted.

'Hello Deborah, hello Jane! Oh, my dears, we've had such a day.' Suzanna was always full of love at the end of those secret trips to the Tunnel Woods that it oozed out of her, spilling and softening until they melted in her warmth and forgave her. But there were neither apologies nor explanations either from radiant Suzanna or loyal Margaret for abandoning the tight knit group, The Needlewick Five. The Henshaw girls and Eleanor

Carney could not understand what had won their friend away.

'What does she do there?' they whispered in the shelter of the willow. 'Why does she keep going to the Tunnel Woods?'

'Mrs Bubb knows,' perceptive Eleanor said, 'but then she would.'

'Why would she?'

'She watches us all. Didn't you know? Anyway, she's been at Roundstones so long.'

'Shall we ask her?'

'Don't be silly! As if she'd tell us.'

'But what do you think Suzanna does there, Eleanor? You must have an idea. Doesn't Margaret say?'

Eleanor was suffering too much from Suzanna's complete defection. 'I don't know and I certainly can't be bothered to find out. If she wants to spend her life traipsing up and down that wretched tunnel, let her. And poor Margaret has to drag after her. Suzanna should be more thoughtful.'

'Perhaps she's got a lover there,' ventured Jane who'd just discovered the word.

'As if she would hide that,' Eleanor said dismissively and went to throw pebbles into the river, first a handful in an angry splatter, then one at a time as she listened for the delicate plop. 'Anyway,' she called, 'you can be sure it won't last. She'll move on to something else before too long. Suzanna can't stick at anything.'

But in this, for once, she was wrong. It was so long before Suzanna was released from her passion that Deborah Henshaw had put up her hair and become absorbed in a social round of picnics and evening parties, and Eleanor Carney had begun to study in earnest, dreaming and scheming to get away from Needlewick to a university. Meanwhile poor Margaret had worn through many a pair of shoes in pursuit of her wayward sister's light footsteps along the path to the Tunnel Woods. It only ended because one day, emerging from the woods by an upper path, the sisters had met a man on horseback. From the moment Simon Theobald's gaze fell on Suzanna's transfigured face, the spell of the Tunnel Woods was broken and so determined and time-consuming was his wooing of her that she never went back.

Looking now at Sophia, the daughter of that union, kneeling in prayer where for eighteen years her mother had knelt each Sunday, Deborah thought: There can be no question of an easy life for you, my lamb, if there's anything at all of your mother in you. But yes, I think one day you will thank Eleanor Gresham for bringing you back here and showing you all this. There are other cards than those your father has dealt you. Your mother has played a fistful and lost the lot, but is that, after all, the worst possible fate for a woman?

10

Sophia took the path to the Tunnel Woods.

The air was moist and heavy but promised warmth later and the river was so still that the rustle of a bird in the undergrowth was startling. She had brought Helen's diary.

Walking was a struggle. Such was her misery that the pain in her heart extended to her stomach, knees and shoulders. It was the extent of her self-delusion that hurt so much; the memory of her feeling of triumph at that wretched wedding, for instance, the consciousness then of her own superior polish and beauty beside her dowdy country cousin. Reading the diary had made the events of that summer return with such clarity: the hot sunny days she had grown to savour once her homesickness diminished; the dragging expeditions along this same path with Helen; the terrible afternoon when she had been lost in the tunnels. The photographs she had taken then were tucked away in her writing box at home, faded, uninteresting prints she had salvaged from Nicholas's desk after his death. There had been one of the clearing in the Tunnel Woods, of course, but it was empty save for Helen seated beneath the tree with her knees clasped to her chest and her head bowed so that her face wasn't visible. All that summer of 1909 Sophia had felt so gloriously good for Helen, such a breath of air, as she filled her cousin's head with new ideas and opened the world for her.

She had of course wondered at Helen's cruelty on that last day at the tunnels – indeed there was much about Helen she had questioned, but then dismissed. Helen after all had seemed such a simple soul, living in a fantasy world with which Sophia had ostensibly sympathised but inwardly treated with incredulity and derision. It was only when Helen failed to reply to her subsequent letters from London that Sophia had become mystified and upset. She had written so revealingly about the situation at home: her mother's desertion, her father's self-absorption and Nicholas suddenly so grown-up he was out of reach. From Helen she had expected sympathy and understanding but received nothing. Now Sophia recognised her cousin's last, belated attempt at self-preservation; now Helen's final hatred for her burned through the shabby covers of the diary.

It was undeserved, Sophia argued to herself, she thought I planned that stupid trick with Michael hiding in the leaves – she might have known I would have had nothing to do with him. But Sophia's conscience rebuked her with the knowledge that her actual betrayal had been more constant and more cruel and had begun the instant she set foot from the train with her shiny hair, smart hat and condescending airs. From the first she had patronised Helen and taken for granted her determination to love and admire this exotic creature from London.

And, as Sophia now acknowledged, she had found Helen's strangeness particularly irritating. Helen had ultimately eluded her because she could retreat to a place where no-one could follow. The diary made clear that she really had believed in those people of hers. Sophia had underestimated the potency of her cousin's imagination. But surely, she thought in self-justification, any sane person would have acted as I did and laughed at her?

Yet the hem of Sophia frock was now wet because she was hurrying along the path to the Tunnel Woods, drawn by curiosity and a sense that her pilgrimage to Needlewick would somehow be incomplete unless she went back there. She felt that she needed to be vindicated by the ordinariness of the clearing.

How far it was. Nothing was familiar, though she passed through coppices and fields which must have been unchanged for generations. In the end she became convinced that she would never reach the Tunnel Woods though she knew that they at least were real. The path, though overgrown, was still used and she wondered who would wish to walk there. Increasingly she felt ill-at-ease; she would even have welcomed Colin's companionship, whilst perversely resenting the intrusion. Not that she would have allowed him to read the diary.

Perhaps Mr Gresham would have come. She blushed at the thought of him reading the diary. They probably all knew, these Needlewick people, how Helen had suffered through her cousin's visit. Undoubtedly Mr Gresham was so tender in his care of Sophia precisely because he knew the diaries would bring her pain. And this brought her back to the same nagging questions. Why had Helen given the diary to Mrs Gresham? And why had she allowed Mrs Gresham to pass it to Sophia?

The knowledge that Mrs Gresham's delicate hands had turned the pages gave Sophia cause to shudder. Yet she had wept most at the entry in the diary that recounted Helen's conversation with Mrs Gresham in the garden of The Grey House. Mrs Gresham, imprisoned in her failing body, had been particularly far-sighted when she spoke of Sophia. '. . . *don't you think, just possibly, that Sophia may have been cruel because she was envious?*'

Sophia was soon tired. Though the sun had not yet broken through the mist, it was already too warm. Then, quite suddenly, she saw that she was nearly at the woods. The trees which had intermittently edged the path grew closer together and ahead the river twisted away amidst dense woodland. But her way was barred by a high fence. The path had been deliberately blocked – and not recently judging by the weathering of the tall stakes and the height of the vegetation which had grown up against them. Sophia stood several feet away as if measuring herself against the obstacle but she did not have the nerve to pit herself against the awkwardness of the fence. As far as she could remember the woods had always been private property and always fenced. This new addition simply closed up their narrow access.

But why is the path so well-used, she thought indignantly? What is the point of anyone coming along here at all when it's a dead end?

The fruitlessness of her expedition and a sense of her own weakness brought tears of frustration as she plodded angrily on. What does it matter? she thought. It is unlike me to bother much about anything. I have read the diary and it has made me uncomfortable but the feeling will pass. Well, let this be an end to it.

But she thought again of Mrs Gresham, who had been dying faster than most, even as she freewheeled her bicycle down the hill or supplied visitors with tea and cake in her sunlit garden. Sophia had been wary of Mrs Gresham for seeing through her own careful veneer to the conceited, uncertain child beneath. Yet for some reason she had thought enough about Sophia to give her the diary. Why, Mrs Gresham?

Michael was fishing from the river bank, his back bent as if he'd nodded asleep, though as Sophia approached she saw that his head was raised, his eyes fixed intently on the river. She was not too disturbed to see him there because she was near Roundstones and had anyway been half expecting him.

'Caught anything?' she called.

He didn't move. 'I could have told you they'd blocked the path.'

She had intended to walk purposefully on but now checked her pace. 'How did you know I'd go there?'

'Where else would you go?'

'Why is the fence there?'

'It's been there for years. Since after you were here last. It's private land. They can do what they like with it.'

She became aware that he was staring at the diary in her hand. He showed no curiosity, only a kind of satisfaction as she hid the notebooks in the fold of her skirt.

'I know a way into the woods,' he said.

'Do you?'

'I'll take you sometime if you like.'

'It's kind of you but I don't think I'll bother. I only wanted a little walk, for old time's sake.'

He shrugged. 'Let me know when you change your mind.'

'Thank you.'

As she walked away she was aware of his gaze on her back. Even after she had rounded a bend in the river she did not feel unwatched.

When she got back to Roundstones and opened the door in the wall she found herself confronted by a little gathering on the lawn with, at its centre, quite at home amidst three middle-aged ladies and a country doctor, Colin.

Retreat was impossible so she adopted a surprised but delighted smile, suitable for the unlooked-for arrival of her betrothed, and held out her hands to him.

'Colin, what a marvellous surprise!'

'I thought I'd come. I'd heard so much about this village and I wanted to save you the train journey home.'

She could tell that he was a little nervous about her possible reaction, but she behaved impeccably. 'My dear, I'm delighted to see you. But poor Aunt Margaret, what a shock for her. You should have let us know. We do have a telephone.'

'Sophia, I don't mind at all,' said Margaret. 'And Lord Kilbride, he says I must call him Colin, but . . . anyway he's not staying here, he says, though of course we'd gladly put him up, I suppose he could have had Helen's room without . . . But he's got friends in Cheltenham, he says, well of course you'd know. But we are all so pleased to meet him.' Aunt Margaret's anxious, gratified smile took in the two ladies from Middlecote Hall who were undoubtedly impressed by this grand visitor.

'You were taking a risk,' Sophia told Colin. 'I could have been gone hours yet. I've been rediscovering my childish haunts.'

'Your aunt and Lady Middlecote have been telling me what an impression you made on Needlewick last time you came. Sophia can't help making an impact on people,' he added fondly.

'If you want tea, Sophia,' said her uncle, 'you'll have to go and get it. This pot's gone cold.'

Sophia retreated thankfully to the kitchen where Mrs Bubb was drinking tea at the kitchen table. Sophia realised that this was the first time she had seen the housekeeper sit down.

'He's come for you then,' Mrs Bubb said.

'You mean Lord Kilbride?' Sophia replied coolly, replenishing the teapot from the kettle. 'Yes, he's very kindly offered to drive me home.'

'I like him.'

'I'm pleased to hear it.'

'I never liked your father.'

Sophia was so surprised by this unwarranted confidence that her response was unguarded. 'I didn't know you'd ever met my father properly.'

'Oh yes, he came here often when he was courting your mother. I knew he wasn't right. He didn't like Needlewick, of course. He wanted to get her away.'

'I think she was ready to leave, don't you Mrs Bubb? I

don't think my mother would have been very happy if she'd stayed here all her life.'

'Happy. What do girls of your age know about happiness?'

Sophia took Colin down to the footbridge where they leaned on the rail and stared down into the clear water, watching the slim reeds bend in the current.

'Helen used to drop sticks in here. She wanted me to play a racing game with her, but I never would. I tried to be so grown-up,' Sophia said.

'You sound sad.'

'I don't mean to be sad. You're here. I'm very flattered you should come all this way for me.'

'I missed you,' he said suddenly. 'You don't know. God I've missed you.'

She stood upright and pressed the base of her spine against the rail. 'You must be far too busy to miss me!'

But he took her fingers and kissed them softly, then held her waist and kissed her cheeks, lips and chin. She obediently clasped his shoulders and responded by opening her lips and teeth, but drew back after a while, oppressed and a little bored. She averted her face and smiled shyly. 'We'll be seen.'

'I don't care who knows that I love you.'

She was used to him telling her he loved her, but for once she felt bowed down by the weight of responsibility the words gave her. She laid her finger on his cheek. 'My love.'

11

The verdict at Middlecote Hall later was that Colin was 'a nice boy, such a nice boy, didn't you think, Jane?'

'Yes, Deborah, I thought so.'

The sisters were at dinner in the vast dining-room where the food lay in over-large dishes on the white table-cloth, waiting for Sir George to snort and wheeze his way through a second helping.

'Of course you won't have met him, George,' persisted Deborah, who always tried to draw him into conversations out of a sense of duty and an even stronger feeling of irritation that anyone could be so incapable of taking an interest in anything other than his own mostly worthless pursuits (claret, cigars, food, guns, horses, felons). 'There's not a trace of the Scot in him – I must ask Sophia about the Kilbride name.'

'You wouldn't expect him to have an accent, surely?' asked Jane.

'Not an accent, but one can usually tell.'

'Did you expect him to be wearing a kilt?'

Deborah's attention was momentarily caught by the size of the load on her brother-in-law's fork.

'Delightful, old-fashioned manners,' she murmured. 'You could tell Lord Kilbride was a gentleman.'

Later, when the sisters were snugly installed in the

sitting-room and Sir George splayed out asleep in his chair, head flung back on the carefully preserved anti-macassar, a half-smoked cigar in the ash-tray, Deborah said: 'Of course Colin Kilbride's not at all right for Sophia.'

'Deborah!'

'He's much too straightforward, don't you think? And she doesn't love him.'

'You have no right to say that, Deborah. I couldn't help thinking how well suited they seemed. He's so fond of her and she does need someone who will cherish her, the poor child, she's had no company but her father's all these years.'

'That may be so but I'm right. He's no use to her, not unless there's more to him than meets the eye.'

'He's a very successful barrister, you know, he's no fool.'

'He may be clever but that's not quite what I meant.'

'You talk about Sophia as if she's very awkward. All the poor girl needs is a little care. She'll soon lose that slightly hard edge she has.'

'So you've noticed it? Even you. She's not awkward, no. What an ugly word. Good Lord, Jane, she's a modern woman. But how will he deal with Suzanna, for instance?'

'*Deal* with her?'

'Sooner or later she'll reappear. Then what? How will Lord Kilbride feel then, in the midst of some dreadful Theobald reunion? Suzanna may even come to Sophia's wedding.'

'I'm sure Lord Kilbride is perfectly capable of dealing with any such eventuality.'

'He'll be charming to Suzanna, as I'm sure he is to everyone. But he won't take her on.'

'Why should he take her on? He's not marrying Suzanna.'

'Oh Good Lord, Jane! Sometimes I think you try to be stupid to irritate me. What I mean is, Suzanna will always be a feature of Sophia's life. She will haunt her, whether she's in London or the other side of Europe. I was always extremely fond of Suzanna, as you know, but I cannot forgive her for abandoning her children. Surely that can never be right, whatever the provocation.' But then, thought Deborah sadly, Suzanna has made a habit of abandoning people. Didn't she abandon us?

When Simon Theobald's presence in Suzanna's life became known to the Henshaw girls, Jane had been bowled over by the romance of it while Deborah had pretended cynicism: 'She doesn't know this man at all. He's simply Suzanna's next phase.' Theobald, a wealthy Londoner looking at some land with a view to building a country retreat, had come across Suzanna and Margaret in the twilight of a May evening and sat above them astride his horse, his eyes never leaving Suzanna's face while Margaret told him the way to Needlewick.

The Henshaw girls had no cause to meet him for several weeks because they were by then far too old to spy from the footbridge or gossip in the sweetshop, on the lookout for Suzanna. Indeed, Deborah was preoccupied with her own marriage at that time, surrounded by lists and trunks and sewing, in her element at last, with little time to listen to Jane's breathless accounts of this most wonderful Needlewick love-affair.

Deborah's own marriage, to stolid Gerald Parditer, a lawyer in the small town of Hippingdean, could hardly be classed as a romance. It was typical that when Deborah's head should have been full of her own nuptials, she should find herself thinking instead of Suzanna with the evening sun on her face as she raised her eyes to meet those of the stranger from London. The Henshaw girls were kept informed of the progress of the courtship by Eleanor who called often to help with Deborah's sewing. And Simon Theobald was invited to Deborah's wedding.

He was a striking figure, very tall beside slender Suzanna, and his handshake was firm and warm. Deborah, impressed by his good looks, particularly by the unusual blue of his eyes and the clear bone structure of nose and chin, glanced sideways at her own brand new husband and thought him rather too short by comparison, and it was a shame that he was already nearly bald. Then, penitent, she squeezed his hand. Parditer was a very good man who showed much affection for his new wife's outspokenness and strength of character. What did a handsome face matter when compared to qualities such as faithfulness and tolerance? But Suzanna was as if shot about with static electricity, her smile brilliant and the contours of her face somehow finer then before, her hair bright beneath a little posy of white roses, one of which, Deborah noticed, still had a drop of dew on its outer petal.

Of course Theobald had taken little interest in the Henshaw girls – although Suzanna introduced them as 'my best friends' – and later, after her third dance with George, Deborah had tiptoed out into the garden and seen Suzanna and Simon Theobald under the vine on the verandah. Simon's hands were cupped under Suzanna's chin; they stood for several moments quite still and then he dipped his head and kissed her. After a while his hands dropped from her face and his arms encircled her so that she was a pinioned doll in his grasp. The force of the kiss, the fusion of their two mouths was never forgotten by Deborah, who later that night received Gerald Parditer's shy advances with a vigour that at first took his breath away.

But sexual energy, thought Deborah, lying in her solitary bed in the guest room at Middlecote Hall, is not enough by itself to sustain a marriage. Poor Gerald is dead and I miss him dreadfully because he overlooked my plainness and the shortcomings of my nature, whereas Theobald was from first to last a very bad choice for Suzanna.

12

Colin drove Sophia home to London on Monday morning. She was not ready to leave Needlewick but had no excuse for staying so sat beside him in a rage because he'd cut short her visit. She had missed his company at times but not enough to outweigh her distress at his intrusion. Besides, she was still raw from her first reading of the diary and had wanted to spend more time at Roundstones in the hope of finding a balm there. Perhaps she might have discovered a way into the Tunnel Woods; it would have been a kind of pilgrimage, an apology to Helen. And she'd had no time to say a proper goodbye to kind Lady Middlecote or her sister, who would consider her sudden departure disrespectful. Worst of all Mr Gresham might think her childish or indifferent, rushing away.

Although she explained nothing of this to Colin, he could not be oblivious to her rigid posture, averted shoulder or silken, monosyllabic replies. Finally he stopped the car where the lane widened by a farm track, took her hand and asked why she was upset. 'Is it anything to do with me?' he added.

His nose was very pink from the rush of air on his face; altogether he looked too boyish and foolish to warrant being hurt.

'Nothing's wrong,' she said. 'I simply didn't want to leave Needlewick.'

'I thought you would have had more than enough of it by now. It's such a tiny place. Your father thought I'd be doing you a favour by rescuing you.'

'Was it on his suggestion that you came?'

'Partly but it didn't take much persuasion.' He picked up her gloved hand and kissed it.

Sophia softened a little. 'I remember last time I didn't want to come home either. But that wasn't because of Needlewick, it was because I was terrified of what I would find at home.'

'What did you find?'

'It's so sordid. Nicholas had warned in this letter, but it was far worse than I expected. Mother was gone, just gone and Father was in a brutal, silent state. Nicholas went back to school. Father wouldn't even let me talk about mother or Needlewick. I somehow came to think that the two events – my being away in Needlewick and her leaving home – were connected.'

'Surely they were.'

'I don't think so. She would have gone off whether I'd been at home or not. She'd had enough of her marriage and wanted to branch out a bit. My father, by the way, would call that a charitable explanation for her behaviour.'

'But your being away must have made it an easier decision for her – she had less responsibility.'

'Colin, she never felt any responsibility for me. She used to produce me like an exhibit at tea parties and before dinner but otherwise she took no real interest in me. Nicholas was the one she loved. We all loved Nicholas.'

There was a sad silence while Colin gently stroked her hand. 'I'm surprised you loved him, if your mother favoured him so much,' he said at last.

'Ah but you see he realised I was left out so tried to compensate. When he was at home he spent hours with me, just talking or walking or playing tennis and when he was away he wrote me letters.' Sophia bit her lip and turned her face aside.

Colin squeezed her hand, restarted the car and drove on through the summer morning. But with every mile Sophia felt more distressed. The wrench away from Needlewick had certainly been too sudden but could surely not account for her depression. A week ago she had been quite content in her father's house, planning her future with Colin. What then? What was it?

Was it that her return to Needlewick and the reading of Helen's diary had given her a glimpse into the brightly lit, albeit sometimes acutely painful world of childhood she had relinquished forever the second her foot touched the doorstep of home after her first Needlewick summer? Then, even as she crossed the threshold from porch to hall, she had sensed her mother was gone. She remembered her father's surprising embrace at the door, and Nicholas waiting on the stairs. After that moment there could be no return. It seemed to Sophia, now speeding home from Needlewick a second time, that she had briefly resurfaced into the light, but was about to plunge again into the murky depths of the pool her father had dug and stocked and tended for her by giving her an expensive but inadequate education, introductions to society, and now a brilliant marriage.

In their first late night conversation, Nicholas, still thin and wan after the measles, had told her that she would be required to choose between her parents. Nicholas's shoulder pressed closer to her as he told her the history of the summer. While Sophia had been stumbling through head-high bracken, waking to bright, bird-noisy mornings or ploughing through musty novels in the Roundstones drawing-room, Nicholas was laid up in bed, an unwilling witness to the final disintegration of their parents' marriage.

'She had started to go out a lot, you know we thought it was with that man, well it wasn't, it was with women; meetings, marches and committees. Father found out because a friend of his saw her one day. She told me, of course, she used to come to my room late at night – I was often awake because being in bed all day I didn't get tired, and she'd tell me about all the excitement of the day. She used to say: "You've seen me, Nicholas, you know me. Aren't I as good as you or your father? So I must have a voice and a vote, we must all have a voice. I'll do anything for that." But he called her a slut. I went down to the library for a book one evening and they were in the hall. He said if she went to any more meetings he would divorce her. She was beside herself. She shouted at him about a morality which allowed her to be a rich man's whore so long as it furthered her husband's career, but stopped her going to meetings which would allow her independence and freedom. And he started hitting her. Smack, smack, smack, smack, back and forward across her cheeks until his ring caught on her hair and tore it down and the side of her face was bleeding. And she didn't resist but cried: "I gave up so much for you. Well, I won't do it again because there's no point. The difference now is I don't love you." And that was it. The next day she left.'

Smack, smack and her hair torn down. Beautiful mother with her gleaming hair and fine skin. She had offered her fragile little body and wild dreams to the suffragists because collective male brutality was a less terrifying enemy than a loveless marriage.

Sophia had met her mother soon afterwards, in the Rose Garden in Regent's Park, at the end of the summer when the grass was sodden and the few remaining blooms hung damp heads and exuded a weary perfume.

Suzanna was waiting on a bench, wearing the heavy brown coat she normally used only for driving. Her hair was dressed in a business-like bun under a neat hat; old brown shoes peeped from beneath a defiantly flirtatious petticoat. Why does she have to dress so dowdily, what is the point? was Sophia's first thought, but, at the same time, her heart turned over at the futility of her mother's gesture, how characteristically she had spent much thought on her appearance, this time in an attempt at self-effacement, and managed only to give her beauty a greater clarity – like an old master in a plain frame. When they kissed, her mother's cheek was soft and fragrant as always. It was Sophia's weakest moment, but passed the instant they moved apart to sit at a distance from each other on the damp seat.

'Mind your skirt, it's not very clean,' Suzanna said. 'I'm sorry we had to meet here – I wanted some privacy.'

Sophia, whilst searching her mother's face for signs of bruising, was awaiting an apology of a different nature.

'How is it at home?' Suzanna asked.

Sophia noticed that her mother was clasping and unclasping her fingers over the handle of her umbrella and was relieved that at least she felt some anxiety for her daughter's well-being. 'What do you think?' she said coldly. 'It's hell without you. Father is furious.'

'And Nicholas?'

'I thought you saw Nicholas quite often.'

'I do, yes, but I think he puts on an act for me and tries to be strong. I don't want to ruin his chances, he must work hard for the new term.'

'Oh, I shouldn't worry. He seems to spend all his time studying. And he'll go away in a couple of weeks.' What about me, she thought, don't you care about me?

Her mother was staring out over the gardens. 'I had to see you, to make sure you understood, Sophia. And to give you a chance, if you want to take it.' Sophia said nothing. 'Nicholas did explain, didn't he, why I had to leave?'

'Not really. I don't understand you. I don't think he does, even.'

'He does, I'm sure. Didn't he tell you what your father did?'

'Why provoke him? He is bound to hate what you are doing.'

Suzanna turned to her suddenly with a pleading, desperate look. 'Sophia, you sound so bitter. I had to do what I felt was right. He was trapping me – I'd just shut my eyes and ploughed on for so many years doing what he wanted.'

'It was what you wanted,' Sophia said harshly. 'You enjoyed every minute of that life.'

'I thought I did at times, if I thought at all, but underneath . . . Sophia, please! Don't let it happen to you. Don't give in to him. You must be free. I'll give you this chance to be free if you come to live with me.'

'I don't even know where you are living,' Sophia said. Inside her head the shutters were slamming fast. Don't offer me insecurity, poverty, dirtying of hands, mother. I don't even want to look.

'I'm staying with a friend for the time being. I have a salary from the Society, just a little, for the administrative work I do. You would carry on at school. There are so many fascinating people for you to meet – and ideas, Sophia.'

'I'm happy as I am, thank you.'

'I thought I was, all I wanted seemed to be your father and Nicholas, and you, and nice things and friends, but it's not enough. I can now influence things, even the way people think. The world is changing, Sophia, for women in particular.'

Sophia turned towards her mother and half raised her hand. Only the memory of the other fingers which had left their mark on that cheek prevented her from slapping her mother's face and saying: *Can't you hear how silly you sound?* But she kept silent.

For a moment Suzanna watched her fearfully, but then seemed to relax as if the fight was over. Did she even look relieved for an instant? Quite calmly she asked: 'Did you like Needlewick?'

'I don't think liking came into it. It's only a village. I miss my cousin.'

'How was Eleanor Gresham?'

'She was well. She's a strange woman.'

'Did you think so?'

'Remote, as if her mind was always on something else.'

'Perhaps it was.'

'Why do you ask about her in particular?'

'She was my best friend. Sometimes I miss her terribly. It is one of my chief regrets that as I grew up I neglected Eleanor. Instead . . .'

'Instead?'

Suzanna was now perched on the edge of the bench, her hands tucked under her thighs, gaze fixed on some indeterminate spot in the rose garden. 'Instead I was drawn away by other things. I had these obsessions as a girl, and if I got an idea in my head there was no stopping me.'

'But can't you see, Mother,' said Sophia, 'it has happened again. You have a new obsession.'

'Did you go to the Tunnel Woods?' asked Suzanna suddenly.

The rose garden was sucked clean of all noise – London traffic, birdsong – instead Sophia was once more in the clearing where Helen sat under the hawthorn tree, face suffused as if with an inner light. 'What about the Tunnel Woods?'

'They were definitely an obsession of mine. I suppose I'd call them a sacred place. I went often and each time, it seemed to me, I came back different. Did you say you had gone there?'

But Sophia couldn't answer. To my mother I am merely a conduit, she thought, for news of Nicholas, Mrs Gresham and Needlewick. There was a long silence, then at last she got up. 'It's very chilly here.'

'Yes, I must go.'

They embraced again, and this time Suzanna's cheek was cold and smelt salty. They promised to write, to see each other soon, but hurried away in different directions.

Unlike on her first return from Needlewick, Sophia's father was not at home, so she and Colin had tea in the drawing-room. Then he left her alone in the big, quiet house. A fire had been lit in her bedroom, but this sign of her father's consideration only increased Sophia's sense of oppression. He's had me fetched back again, she thought. Here I am, all ready to dress in my best and go down to dinner with him. On life goes.

At Roundstones now the tea things would be cleared away, her aunt would be underfoot in the hot kitchen helping Mrs Bubb with the dinner and Sophia might have been lying on her narrow bed gazing out at a wide sky. I was only a guest there, she thought sadly, I didn't belong. She dressed for dinner, stifling tears which had no apparent cause and a yearning which seemingly had no object.

But the enforced intimacy of another meal with her father proved intolerable. Sophia, dressed in oyster-pink lawn, sat on his right. Pleasantries were exchanged; the Needlewick relatives all accounted for. 'And thank you,

Father, for having a fire lit in my room, it was most thoughtful.' She asked after his business, and then found nothing further to say. And she took no comfort from the knowledge that she had only two more months until she would leave the house and be Colin's wife. *Father's face will simply be replaced with another's* she thought, panic-stricken.

Unexpectedly, certainly without premeditation, she heard herself say: 'I've decided against marrying Colin. At least, I think I'll postpone it.'

The words sounded so matter of fact that she was surprised by their impact on her father and had taken another mouthful of melon before she realised that he was sitting quite still, one hand on his napkin, another still holding his fork.

'I hope not,' he said at last.

'Yes, I hope you don't mind.' Fortunately she did not giggle at this last-stated wish, although she was amazed by her own impudence.

There was another silence. 'Has Colin any views on this subject?'

'I haven't mentioned it to him. I haven't quite made up my mind.' *I actually only thought all this up in the last three minutes.*

'May I ask why you have changed your mind?'

'Various reasons, I think. I don't love him enough is one. I think I'd make him pretty miserable, therefore. And I suppose I don't want to be married at the moment. I feel as if I haven't had a chance to live at all yet.'

'Do you know how foolish you sound?' he asked suddenly.

'Do I? Is the fact that I'd make Colin miserable foolish, Father?' Her voice wobbled. The prospect of Theobald's disapproval had always terrified her. She clutched at remaining shreds of control by finishing her melon before quietly leaving the room.

Why? she thought, as she plodded upstairs. Sophia, what have you done? For it was done. Colin might have been able to talk her out of a wild decision; her father's frigid affront only scored fierce lines under her change of heart. Having taken the plunge she could not go back. It had not been so terribly difficult, after all, to do the unforgivable. Sophia had always sensed that her father's power lay in his great charm and in his ability to withdraw it completely. She had known that almost anything would be better than incurring the full weight of his wrath. When she returned from Needlewick in the late summer of 1909 to be presented with a clear choice – his goodwill or her mother's unreliable care – she had chosen the former. Now she had neither.

She could not bring herself to speak to Colin either that night or during their next meeting. In an absurd way it did not seem relevant that she was not after all intending to marry him. After all, she was accustomed to talking to him with her mind elsewhere so it would be going against months of habit actually to tell him what she was thinking.

She planned to write to him – eventually. Meanwhile her father subjected her neither to pleading, nor rages. Only silence. An icy draught blew through the house.

Sophia's hands and feet were chilled as if she were physically unable to withstand such an absence of affection. At night she lay in bed with rigid limbs and sore eyes until too exhausted not to sleep. Only Nicholas might have protected her. But she had waved goodbye to Nicholas once too often.

Out of desperation she wrote to her mother, care of a relief organisation in Zurich, an address received from Suzanna at Christmas. In the letter she wished her mother well, and said that she planned to terminate her engagement to Colin, but found she had no other plans for her immediate future (she did not write: for her life) and wondered whether she might join Suzanna for a while. Immediately after sealing the envelope she rushed off a note to her cousin Helen Callwood, offering to visit her in Cambridge. Unable to articulate reason, Sophia offered none. In her heart she knew that she sought Helen's forgiveness and, with it, comfort.

But she sent both letters with a kind of hopelessness, convinced that she was sending them into voids from which there would be no reply.

Still she said nothing to Colin. It was as if she was living at such a distance from everybody that whether or not she was engaged, or to whom, did not matter at all.

Colin was a frequent guest at dinner and one night, during dessert, Theobald asked, 'And what is your response to Sophia's interesting new approach to her engagement, Kilbride?'

His would-be son-in-law as usual responded eagerly. 'Sir?'

Sophia laid down her knife.

'I assume she's told you of the new arrangements,' Theobald added lightly.

Colin's boyish gaze was now directed humorously at Sophia. 'Let me guess. Gretna Green?'

Sophia took a peach and rolled it across her palm. 'We'll talk about it later,' she said at last.

Theobald's fruit knife twisted into a grape, deftly removed two pips and deposited them onto the side of his plate. 'My daughter is a cold fish, Kilbride. You may well be glad to be shot of her after your initial shock. In that respect she's very like her mother – you can never be quite sure what she's thinking. Best steer clear of a woman like that.'

Colin still did not look like a drowning man, his tone was amused. 'I think Sophia and I understand each other pretty well.'

'We thought of christening her Suzanna, but I decided not to in the end. Even then, when I had no cause to be suspicious of my wife, I did not want to create another female in her image.'

'I thought you loved Mother very much then,' Sophia said. 'You'd only been married a few years.'

'Oh, love, Sophia! You're such a child. I was always falling in and out of love, young men are like that, love is on their minds much of the time. I ended up with your mother but it might have been any one of a number of young women; all beautiful, blooming and smooth-haired.'

'Then why choose my mother? Why uproot her from Needlewick and bring her here?'

'It was the challenge, Sophia. She seemed so fixed, so gloriously a part of her home. I thought, Let's see if I can make her mine.'

Colin said, 'Needlewick seemed a very pleasant little place, I thought.'

'Yes, you should have spent part of your honeymoon there. That would have been by far the best plan. Then Sophia need not have gone there on her own. It would have been too late.'

'Sir? Too late?'

'Christ, Suzanna was rotten. And look at my daughter. She has no sense of duty or gratitude.'

Sophia's hands were now folded on her lap. 'What my father's trying to tell you, Colin, is that I've had second thoughts about our engagement. Nothing definite. I just think we should talk about it, perhaps postpone it for a while.'

'I see.'

'Perhaps, if Father would excuse us, we could go now. I'd like to talk to you alone.'

'Let the boy finish his meal. Give him a few more moments' pleasure.'

Sophia stood, expecting Colin to follow her from the room. But Colin stayed in his chair and Theobald reached for the port.

13

Helen's reply was remarkably prompt – Sophia recognised the girlish handwriting at once. She wrote very briefly that there was no need for Sophia to visit Cambridge as Helen had an engagement in London at the end of the month and would call one morning. Sophia wrote back more warmly and said how delighted she would be to meet again.

During the ten days she waited for Helen no word came from her mother. Her father, as expected, showed no sign of softening. He had never relented towards Suzanna so Sophia presumed that he could, if necessary, maintain this air of disapproval for the rest of his life. She made a point of waiting until she knew he'd left the house before going down to breakfast, and he frequently dined out. When they did eat together they rarely spoke but listened to the sound of each other's chewing and swallowing. Any conversation Sophia tried to instigate was met by polite but monosyllabic responses.

Once she embraced him. Before she left the dining-room she put her arms round him and murmured: 'I'm sorry I've caused you so much pain, Father.' He sat rigidly until she had withdrawn, then said: 'When it's convenient perhaps you will let me know the new date of your marriage, or whether you've decided to call it off completely.'

She had planned her pathetic little gesture since the early hours of the morning and his rebuff was crushing. But still she could not break free of him; she had been dependent on his goodwill for too long.

Colin was never at home when she called so she made an appointment at his chambers. She knew his rooms quite well, and while waiting in an ante-room had cause to wonder at the difference one conversation at dinner could make. In the past, when she'd arranged to meet here, he would have been hovering at the window, watching for her, even when with a client. Hurrying along the uneven pavement outside, she would always look for him and wave. That afternoon she was kept waiting several minutes, although she had been punctual, and when he at last ushered her in, he gestured to the chair opposite his desk, not, as formerly, drawing up a stool and sitting at her knee so that he might kiss her cheek or hand once in a while.

She had not expected that her rejection of him would cause him such hurt. Formerly buoyant, rather school-boyish, unashamedly and openly affectionate, he was now very composed, closed down, neatly dressed, hair tidy, face pale. He had retreated far inside himself to lick his wounds. At last she realised the enormity of what she had done. She did not blame herself for breaking the engage-ment – but for entering into it so selfishly in the first place.

He watched her intently, as if she were some danger-ous zoological specimen; eyes narrowed, expression wary.

She said: 'I came to apologise for that dreadful dinner. It was unforgivable of my father to interfere in that way. It must have seemed to you appallingly cruel.'

'I had to know. It was only fair. In fact I have been wondering at what point you would have broken the news if left to your own devices.'

'I don't know, I couldn't bring myself to,' she said, hating herself for the lie, but how could she admit that she had been far too preoccupied to show him any consideration? 'It all seems so unreal, even now. If you asked me what I really wanted I wouldn't be able to say, or why I became unsure of my own mind. It's so silly, isn't it?'

Taking up his fountain pen, he turned it over and over.

'Colin, I'm so sorry!' she said. 'I didn't want to hurt you like this!'

He shrugged: 'That's all right.' Now that he had retreated so far the enormity of what she'd lost struck her; so much generous, undemanding love. 'Colin, I would have been no good for you,' she said, 'you're too fine for me.'

He was angry at last. 'Whip yourself with that if you like. You know it's nonsense. The thing is you don't love me and never have.'

'Do you want us to finish completely?' she asked.

'If you like. It's up to you.'

'Please don't say that. We're in it together. Shall we postpone our decision for a few weeks? What do you think?'

'What's the point?'

'So we can be sure we're doing the right thing. It seems so dreadful to throw it all away.'

'If you like – you can let me know what you want in a few weeks.'

'And you? You must let me know – you have every right. Your feelings might change too.'

He got up abruptly, helped her into her coat and showed her to the door.

Life in her father's house was intolerable. Sophia's nerves were tortured by her relentless agonising. Where should she go? What should she do? Why had she thrown away her future with such a good man?

She went to her writing box – formerly her mother's, it was small and impractical but had a lock and key – and took out her sheaf of Needlewick photographs. They had been badly taken and, caring little for them after they were developed, she had crammed them together so that their edges were crushed. But now she held them up, one after another, and studied them as if for comfort.

But in the one of Mrs Gresham for instance, her subject's face was so ill-defined that she might have been any woman in any garden. And why had she never bothered to photograph Mr Gresham? Presumably because he had seemed insignificant at the time, or was tucked away in his study. The photographs of Round-stones were better: here were Uncle Harry and Aunt Margaret and Helen, who was smiling eagerly. Remembering the diary, Sophia could not look at that smile for long. Those of the clearing held no magic. She had photographed the woods carelessly, too impatient to focus the lens and too inexperienced to manage the light.

Yet she loved to handle the photographs because they were a direct link with Needlewick.

She realised that there was only one place where she might recover, make decisions, even ask for advice, perhaps from Mr Gresham. She wrote to her Aunt Margaret of the postponed engagement and asked whether she might return to Needlewick for a little while to think clearly about her future.

The morning Helen was due to visit was cold and blustery, foreshadowing the coming of autumn. Remembering how Helen loved flowers, Sophia filled the vases in the drawing-room with chrysanthemums. She spent an hour selecting and discarding clothes as being either too showy or too expensive and finally chose a dress she'd not worn for years. Because it reminded her of summer days in the war, she disliked the dress but it seemed appropriate for Helen's visit.

The diaries and photographs were laid out on her bed. Sophia thought that after lunch they might go up and look at them together. Perhaps Helen would laugh at her own former intensity and old fantasies. How else could she be asked to forgive the past?

Helen arrived at eleven precisely. Sophia stood at the drawing-room window and listened to the murmur of voices in the hall, quick steps on the stairs, the opening of the door. 'Miss Callwood.'

'Helen.' Sophia crossed the room, took Helen's arm

and kissed her cheek. 'How lovely to see you. Please, sit down. Your jacket?'

Helen was very composed. 'I said I'd keep it. I can't stay long.'

'Coffee?'

'No, thank you.'

'Nothing at all?'

Helen had retained the ability to be very still. Sophia poured coffee for herself with shaking hands, her carefully prepared conversation now useless. For want of any other words, she said: 'I like your hair, a bob suits you.'

In fact Helen looked terrible; short hair, badly cut, only accentuated the roundness and pallor of her face. She had been plump as a girl, now she had the figure of a matron and her calf-length brown skirt revealed thick ankles and heavy shoes. Her eyes, now hidden behind thick spectacles, were those of a complete stranger.

Sophia had expected to find her cousin reserved but Helen replied calmly: 'It's much easier to manage shorter hair when one has so little time.' She examined the flowers, porcelain, loose covers. 'It's a lovely room.'

'Of course, everything is terribly old. We've hardly changed it since mother left.'

'How is your mother?'

'When I last heard she was well, I believe.' Shame made Sophia blush. 'I'm not very good at keeping in touch with her. She travels so much. I was glad to find your parents in good health when I was in Needlewick.'

'They seem all right. I don't have much chance to visit them.'

'Tell me about your work, Helen. It's such a mystery to me. I never thought you'd be interested in mathematics.'

'What did you think I'd do?'

'I don't really know, but you seemed more artistic.' Phrases of your diary sing through my memory night and day.

'Well it's more useful to be practical. I find mathematics a great challenge.' Though Helen's tone was not rude or repressive, Sophia was chilled. Helen spoke as if to a passing acquaintance, a fellow passenger on the train perhaps.

'And what's it like living in the university? It would frighten me to be among all those great brains.'

'I suppose I felt daunted at first but one gets used to it. I'm in my element there.'

Your element, Sophia thought. Helen, what about the Tunnel Woods, the cow parsley in the lane, the girl with no hat who made daisy chains and raced sticks in the stream?

'Don't you miss Needlewick at all?'

'At first I did, but not now. There's nothing for me to do in the village, you see. And of course Mrs Gresham's death was a great blow. I couldn't have got anywhere without her encouragement.'

'I wish I'd known her better. She seems to have been a remarkable woman. Everyone in Needlewick misses her so much.'

'She was the one who particularly wanted me to go to Cambridge. You know she would have gone there herself if she hadn't started to be ill.'

'I didn't know that.'

'No, she didn't tell me for years. Anyway, now she's gone I'm afraid I don't have a lot in common with anyone else at home.' There was an uncomfortable pause and then she asked: 'What about you, you're engaged, aren't you?'

'Was. I was. Now – we're not sure.'

Helen shrugged. 'What would you do instead? How do you spend your time? You must feel the loss of Nicholas.'

'I do.'

'I should have liked to meet him. I envied you having a brother.'

'Actually, I miss him dreadfully. He somehow managed to stay close to all of us when the family split up. I had to choose, he didn't.'

'It was a wicked war.' Helen said suddenly.

Sophia looked at her in surprise. 'Why do you say that?'

'Don't you think so?'

'Not really.' Sophia had never judged the war at all. She asked impulsively: 'Would you like to see Nicholas's room?'

Helen looked astonished: 'If you'd like to show me.'

'There's nothing really there, we cleared it all away. There wasn't much to tidy, he was terribly organised.'

'Please – I'd like to have a look.'

Sophia's skin was prickling with embarrassment as they climbed the stairs. When she opened the door, Nicholas's room looked so ordinary – an over-tidy bedroom in a large town-house. Whatever would Helen think?

But Helen walked confidently into the room and sat on the bed. 'There's a great dearth of young men at Cambridge. There must be so many empty bedrooms like this one across the country. Did he write to you much? I remember you were always getting letters while you were staying with us.'

'He tried to protect me too much then, and during the war. His letters were so cheerful always. But because he never wrote about how it really was I suppose in the end he shut me out. I'd rather have known the worst. When he died I felt I didn't know him properly at all. That was part of the loss.'

'Of course.' Sophia noticed Helen glance at her watch. 'I'm meeting a friend for lunch at one in Oxford Street.'

'I thought we would have lunch here.' Nothing of importance had been said, time was slipping away. 'I'm sorry it's been so long since we've been in touch.'

Helen smiled politely.

'It was really Mrs Gresham's death that made me write to you,' Sophia said desperately.

'Yes, I imagined there was some connection.'

'She left me your diary.'

'Yes, she said she would.' There was no hint of confusion or self-consciousness, just a little grimace. 'I shudder to think what I'd written.'

'Don't you remember?'

'Not really. I expect a whole lot of stuff about you. I remember keeping a diary during that time you came to stay. I was so thrilled to have a visitor.'

'I thought you'd have hated me reading your private diaries.'

'I haven't really considered the matter. It all seemed so foolish. I couldn't understand Mrs Gresham but it would have been churlish to refuse. Her letter asking my permission to give the notebooks to you was so anxious and urgent, quite unlike her, and I could tell by the writing she was far from well.'

'But I upset you so much, when I came to stay. Surely you remember.'

She laughed. 'Did you? I expect I was jealous. You must have seemed very exotic to me. Actually I think you were probably good for me. I couldn't stand Needlewick after you'd gone, I had to get away, it seemed so parochial so I went off to school. The Greshams were terribly kind and helped with the fees.' She got up and walked to the door. 'I'm afraid I really mustn't be late. My friend would be rather annoyed.'

'Helen, what about the Tunnel Woods? Did you ever go back?'

'Go back?'

'Don't you remember what happened there?'

Helen was on the stairs and did not hesitate. 'Of course I remember the Tunnel Woods. I went for walks there sometimes, though I wasn't supposed to. But it was quite a trek. In the end I got lazy I suppose.' Her gloves were on. She was by the front door.

'Would you like to have the diaries back now?' asked Sophia.

'Good Lord, no! I should throw them away if I were you.'

In a moment she'd be gone, she was turning away. But suddenly she took her spectacles off and polished them with a handkerchief. Briefly her gaze met Sophia's and in that moment Sophia saw a glimmer of the remembered Helen in her dreamy grey eyes, once lit by an unreachable inner candle.

'I hadn't realised you were short-sighted,' said Sophia.

'I am, very. I didn't realise myself 'til I went away to school. I must have lived in a blur for years. I'm surprised no-one noticed, including my father.' She held out her hand. 'Thank you for writing to me.'

After she'd gone the hall was exactly as before, dim and silent. Helen's visit had made no impression.

'I am going back to Needlewick, Father.'

No reply.

'You don't mind?'

No reply.

'Have you any message for Aunt Margaret?'

No reply.

Sophia no longer feared him. She was cut off from him and everyone else. It was as if she were a fragment of gossamer, floating up and away, and if he caught her, would she care?

'I still haven't heard from Mother, though I've made several enquiries and written to a forwarding address.'

At last he laid down his knife and fork. 'Why did you write to your mother?'

'Because she is my mother. I have neglected her long enough; it is inexcusable of me.' Her father's blue stare had the effect of making her say far more than she had intended. 'And there was that diary, left me by Mrs

Gresham. I wanted to ask Mother about her childhood in Needlewick and a place called the Tunnel Woods.'

The Tunnel Woods. The name fell into the great chasm between them and created another silence. But as Sophia left the room she glanced back at her father and saw that his cheek was wet with tears.

14

Margaret Callwood wrote that Sophia would have to postpone her intended visit to Needlewick because Mrs Bubb had been taken ill, she'd had a stroke and required constant nursing.

Sophia tore up the letter, took the first available train to Cheltenham and from there a cab. She had burnt all her boats in London – if Needlewick too was burning, then so be it, she would rather go down on the Roundstones' ship.

During the journey she thought of the people she had wronged, notably Helen and Colin. Helen had been so guarded during her visit, perfectly in control, disingenuous. It was impossible to tell what she actually felt for Sophia, perhaps only indifference or perhaps, remembering the old hurt, she had put up a barrier. Either way, Sophia had found Helen's lack of interest wounding.

And Colin? Her initial anguish at his suffering had been replaced by weariness. What could she do about him? She obviously did not have the ability to make anyone happy, being so unhappy herself. In fact she envied purposeful Helen with her ink-stained fingers and myopia; she might be a blue-stocking but at least she had knowledge and an occupation. What am I, thought Sophia, but a former fiancée, former sister and, to all intents and purposes, a former daughter?

But as the train neared Cheltenham she was preoccupied with more immediate problems and grew frightened by her audacity at travelling to Needlewick expressly against her aunt's wishes. What should she do if she were turned away, though she knew such dramatic action by her kindly uncle and aunt was unlikely. During the slow drive to Needlewick her courage dwindled with every twist in the lane. Not wishing to give her relatives the means to send her home at once, she dismissed the cab at the bridge in the village and walked up the hill, carrying her own bags. By the time she arrived at Roundstones rain was falling in heavy droplets and she had to struggle with both luggage and umbrella. After ringing the bell she stood dripping forlornly in the porch for a long time before anyone answered.

Aunt Margaret could not disguise her horror at the sight of Sophia. 'Didn't you get my letter?'

'What letter, aunt?'

'I wrote several days ago. Surely I posted the letter, perhaps I forgot. I can't have you here, Mrs Bubb is sick, the house is all upside down. One of the Makepeace girls . . . but she's so lazy . . . and there's the nurse to feed. I can barely manage.'

'I'm so sorry. Oh dear!'

'Come in now and I'll make some tea. How did you get here?' She peered hopefully up the lane for some means of transport to carry her niece away.

The drawing-room was chilly and unused. Outside the garden was subdued by rain, the roses well past their best bloom. Despite her aunt's letter, Sophia had expected Roundstones to be more or less the same. Now she realised how far she was intruding on a family crisis.

Nevertheless, she determined not to be sent away. On Sophia's previous visit Aunt Margaret had been attentive and sympathetic, deeply interested in her niece's life and welfare. Now she could think of nothing but Mrs Bubb who was after all only a servant. The tea was weak and there was no cake. 'We'll have to see what your uncle says. He might be able to run you back to the station.'

'I couldn't ask him to do that.'

'Perhaps Mr Gresham then. He's very good.'

'Aunt, if you can bear it, I'll stay here for the night and then in the morning I'll make my own arrangements. I'm dreadfully sorry to intrude on you like this. But I promise I'll be no trouble, might even be of some help.'

Margaret looked at her without hope.

'Is there nothing I could do?' Sophia said.

'Perhaps you could sit with Mrs Bubb while I get on with the supper. Susan Makepeace really is so unused to the kitchen still, and the nurse is very particular about her food. She usually has a break about this time.'

As they climbed the two flights of stairs to Mrs Bubb's room Margaret whispered: 'I asked if she'd like to be brought downstairs but the idea seemed to agitate her. She's occupied the same room since her husband died about thirty years ago.'

'You're very good to her.'

'Sophia, she's been with my family since she was twelve. This is her home. Nothing can be too much trouble.'

The room was very close and smelt of sick, old flesh. It was small and bare – Mrs Bubb had collected few belongings over the years.

'We think she can hear and see,' said Aunt Margaret, 'but she can't speak or move so we're not sure.'

When told that Sophia was to sit with her for a little while, the mound on the bed made no sign. The patient was turned every half hour or so, and now lay on her back with her eyes closed. Left alone, Sophia perched on the hard chair by the window and looked anxiously at the still figure, then, intimidated, she turned away and was startled by the view commanded by this second floor room. From under the eaves at Roundstones she could see west along the valley of the Needle for several miles, even perhaps as far as the Tunnel Woods – yes, there were woods away in the distance. Sophia followed the line of the river – she could even, in places, make out the path.

And because Mrs Bubb's bedroom was at the corner of the house there was another, larger window overlooking the garden, Middlecote Hall and, away to the east, Needlewick. Altogether Mrs Bubb had a most comprehensive outlook. Sophia wondered how often she and Helen had been watched unnoticed from these windows.

She crossed to the bed and looked into the housekeeper's face; the eyes were now open and seemed to stare directly up at Sophia who smiled uneasily. Mrs Bubb made no response except perhaps for a slight flicker of her steady gaze. She was lying on her back and the heavy flesh around her mouth and nose fell back, leaving the mouth slightly open, with a dribble of saliva at one corner.

'I hope you're comfortable,' Sophia murmured and returned to her chair. 'Perhaps next time I'll bring a book,' she added more confidently, 'and read aloud to you.'

The silence was intimidating but Sophia continued: 'I was so sorry to find you were ill. My aunt wrote to me but I didn't get the letter in time.' The words sounded hollow in the still room.

There were no books except a red-bound Bible. A few photographs stood on the mantelpiece and the chest-of-drawers, too far away for Sophia to study and too near the bed to be approachable.

Instead she looked at her hands and feet, the hem of her dress, flecks of dust on the old carpet; the room was so neat and clean there were few other distractions. She tiptoed again to the bed but crept away because Mrs Bubb now had her eyes shut.

At last, after three quarters of an hour, her aunt returned and ushered her out. 'Your uncle's here and will be up to have a look at her in a while. We've put your bags in your room – supper should be ready quite soon. It was really very kind of you, dear.'

After hurrying downstairs and closing the door of her room behind her, Sophia gave a nervous little giggle. She shivered because her room was cool after the warmth of the sickroom.

Yet she would do it again if need be. She might even perhaps be of use to her aunt. This was such a novel idea that she laughed out loud.

Harry Callwood actually encouraged Sophia to stay at Roundstones, perhaps motivated by the fact that during the very plain evening meal Margaret was so overstrained and flustered. 'I'm afraid the potatoes aren't quite cooked. Oh – is the meat tough? That girl doesn't understand the oven yet. She tries very hard but in some ways she's like the mother.' She paused, then told her husband, 'Sophia says she can get a cab in the morning.'

'Isn't she staying?' he asked mildly.

'Harry, she can't. I've so much work. I'm so sorry dear, but Mrs Bubb takes up all my time.'

'I'd like to help,' Sophia said tentatively.

'There now, I think that would be a jolly good idea,' said the doctor. 'We'd hoped Helen might have come home but she's writing an important paper, she tells us. Sophia could be a great help, Margaret, and she'd cheer us all up.'

'But Sophia can't cook or clean,' Margaret cried, forgetting her usual deference. 'What could she do?'

'I can sit with Mrs Bubb. I can help with the house. I have lived through a war, you know.'

There was a tiny pause as these last words had their due effect.

'Of course, dear, but are you sure that's what you want? Is it the best thing for you – your father, and then your engagement, we were so sorry . . . such a nice man.'

Sophia knew that Margaret did not want her at Roundstones; she regarded her as an intruder, and did not believe she could be of any help. So to prove her worth she insisted on clearing the meal by herself. Too tired to resist, her aunt went quite willingly to rest in the drawing-room. Sophia found the Makepeace girl in the kitchen, clumsy and pale with her mother's huge, protruding eyes. She had finished her own meal and sat at the table, pushing her spoon round her bowl. The kitchen was so untidy Sophia could not think where to begin.

'I'll clear the table. You fill the sink and make a start, Susan.'

Neither of them spoke again. Sophia considered that when she had tidied the dining-room she had done enough. 'We'll have coffee when you've finished,' she told the servant, and fled.

Coffee never appeared. When Sophia went back to the kitchen Susan had gone, leaving the room moderately neat. Sophia went to bed. Sleep came easily in Needlewick with only owls to disturb the quiet of the night.

15

Sophia developed a relationship with Susan Makepeace. With plenty of admiration and encouragement the girl worked quite fast so Sophia spent some time each day chivvying her round the house.

Occasionally Sophia went shopping for her aunt and once a day, in the late afternoon, she sat with Mrs Bubb. Though she dreaded these sessions, she regarded them as the fee she must pay for being allowed to stay in Needle-wick. So she learnt the tasks of turning the patient and giving her dribbles of water. Within a couple of days she was allowed to sit in the sickroom by herself from five to seven each evening. Her greatest fear was that Mrs Bubb might either die or speak on her watch and, to avoid either eventuality, she asked her uncle if reading aloud to the patient might be appropriate; she had a superstitious belief that no-one could die while she was reading to them. There was very little of interest in the bookshelves at Roundstones but eventually she chose a volume of Grimm's fairytales, very closely printed and with macabre pen and ink illustrations. Thereafter, whenever Mrs Bubb had her eyes open, Sophia read stories to her, one after another in a slow, clear voice. A vicious world was created in that sickroom, of blood falling on white flesh, of fairies and giants, dark forests, noble princes and talking beasts. Sophia never knew what Mrs Bubb thought of these stories, or even if she heard them but for herself she found them fascinating.

Visitors came frequently to Roundstones. Lady Jane Middlecote called daily, as did the new vicar, a loud-voiced, helpless churchman with red skin and thin mousy hair. Margaret had many friends in the district and Sophia received a good deal of praise as she handed the tea cups: 'So kind of dear Sophia to come and help her aunt.' Always there were polite enquiries after Helen – unspoken were the words: 'She should be here.' Nobody mentioned Suzanna.

Sophia had plenty of time to herself, indeed the days seemed very long. She walked and read but did not much relish her own company. In the end, for want of other occupation, she took to writing long letters to Colin, full of village gossip and fairy tales. At first she received no reply and expected none but after a while he began to write notes from his office or from court. Sometimes he drew sketches of fellow lawyers, or ushers. She began to watch for the post, but was disappointed even when there was a letter from him; she craved affection, not pen-sketches. She examined his signature, *Yours, Colin*. He had always before written *With all my love*. She also wrote dutiful notes to her father to maintain a fragile link with him.

On Friday evening Mr Gresham called to ask if she would like to take a walk with him the following day. 'I thought you might be lonely here,' he said, with his usual diffidence.

At Sophia's suggestion they took the path to the

Tunnel Woods. She was irresistibly drawn to them and frequently walked that way alone, though never far.

They began by talking about Mrs Bubb; it was a safe topic and a natural one.

'Do people usually recover from strokes?' Sophia asked, sweeping the leaves of the willow with her fingers. The prognosis of Mrs Bubb's illness was a forbidden subject at Roundstones.

'Your uncle would know better than I do. I think age, weight and general health have much to do with it.'

Mr Gresham was dressed smartly in a light summer suit. Sophia, visualising him alone in a gentleman's outfitters, felt her heart contract. He was such an unassuming man; how could he choose himself a suit?

'Aunt Margaret is so fond of her, it'll be a terrible blow if she dies.'

'Of course Mrs Bubb knew your mother and aunt when they were babies.'

'Did you ever meet my grandparents, Mr Gresham?'

'I do remember them, your grandmother in particular. Eleanor always said Suzanna was very like her mother. I think the little girls were left to Mrs Bubb a good deal.'

Sophia became aware that he was performing a dance behind her in an attempt to take the side of the path nearest the river. She made room for him and said, 'I find it frightening to sit in the room with poor Mrs Bubb. She is so quiet, yet I feel she knows a lot about me, from when I was here before.'

'I expect she does. And she was devoted to your mother.'

'Everyone seems to have been fond of my mother. I feel now that I scarcely knew her.'

She realised, too late, that he would probably dislike her display of emotion, but he said, 'I did not know her very well, and only briefly before her marriage. But you could never forget her, never. And Eleanor used to talk about her very often.'

He spoke his wife's name calmly, and Sophia adopted the same unsentimental tone. 'It's always puzzled me why they didn't keep in touch if they were such good friends. I would have thought Mrs Gresham would have been sympathetic to mama when she left my father.'

'My wife was deeply attached to her. She was very sad when Suzanna went away from Needlewick but Suzanna hardly ever wrote to her. I think maybe that's why she gave you the diary. For your mother's sake.'

Sophia was surprised that he should mention the diary after his reluctance to discuss it before. They had come to a part of the river where the water trickled softly round smooth rocks. Although the day was overcast and chill she suggested they might sit for a while. 'I used to come here with Helen, I told her off for dabbling her feet in the water because I said it was considered so unfashionable to have brown feet.'

It was peaceful by the river with Mr Gresham. He had an air of tranquillity about him that day, as if the shyness and distress which she had seen in him before had diminished to reveal an inner core of strength. So she dared.

'Mr Gresham, you said you had read Helen's diary. Helen wrote about "her people", do you remember? And

I was cruel, I laughed at her. But your wife, I just wondered, did she know about the Tunnel Woods? You see I don't understand. Before I read the diary I couldn't think why Helen tried to deceive me by inventing all that stuff. At the time I thought she was trying to impress me. Then I read the diary and realised she did believe in her people, whatever she meant by them. And then, meeting her recently in London, I felt as if she didn't care one way or another about the diary because none of it meant anything to her any more. So I came back because I don't understand how she could have forgotten, and because I want to know what the truth is.'

Mr Gresham was perched uncomfortably on a boulder, bare-headed. Watching his face she realised that he had suggested this walk because of the diary and had been waiting for the right moment. 'Eleanor wanted to go back to the Tunnel Woods,' he said, 'but by the time she told me about them it was too late. I could not get her there on this rough path in her weakened state. It was too much for her. So I went by myself, having read the diary.'

'Did you go to the clearing?'

He smiled. 'I tried but I couldn't find it. There was the path and the tunnels, but then, once away from the tunnels, there seemed to be no way through the bracken. I presume because Helen had stopped going there it was overgrown.'

'Yes.' Sophia's voice was weak with disappointment.

'You see, it was because of those woods that your mother fell out with Eleanor or so Eleanor always thought.'

'Did they go there too?'

'They all went. They were quite a little gang. The Needlewick Five they called themselves. I didn't live here when I was a boy but I remember meeting this group of girls at Christmas parties. There was your mother and your aunt, and the Henshaw girls, now Lady Middlecote and her sister Deborah Parditer and Eleanor. Eleanor was in some ways the odd one out, as you can imagine, but she and your mother were very close. Eleanor kept notes your mother wrote to her when they were little girls. They had their own code. She made me destroy them before she died.'

The river flowed clear and untroubled and a bird flew swiftly from the opposite bank. Minnows flicked from under the rocks. 'Did Aunt Margaret mind about their friendship?'

'Perhaps a little. She loved Suzanna very much. I think they all did. Even I fell for her until I realised Eleanor was the one for me.'

More than twenty-five years of river had flowed past these same boulders since Mr Gresham had last seen Suzanna. Sophia had a photograph of her mother taken during her engagement, dressed in white, with masses of fair hair piled above her delicate neck.

'So why did Mother and Eleanor fall out? It seems so sad. I think Mother must have needed her friends so much over the years.' Sophia was gripped by such pain and remorse and longing to see her mother that she could not remain still. So she leant forward and trailed her hand in the water.

'They found the clearing,' said Mr Gresham. 'All of them. They used to roam about the countryside and one day they found the clearing and after that nothing was the same. Your mother became secretive and took to going off on her own or rather with just Margaret. Finally, after much persuasion she confided that something had happened in the clearing and she had to go back there often. She never said what for. Eleanor was very sad at being excluded. I imagine the Henshaw girls were also upset but Deborah was slightly older, nearly ready to come out. Your aunt and her sister grew very close because Margaret was allowed to go with Suzanna as far as the tunnels.'

'So Aunt Margaret must have understood about Helen's obsession with the Tunnel Woods.'

'Very probably. But your aunt has always had a somewhat distracted nature, you can never tell what she's really thinking or noticing. Perhaps she was even proud, or thought it inevitable, that Helen should follow in Suzanna's footsteps.'

His knuckles were white with cold, Sophia noticed. They began to walk back, she very concerned for him in his light suit.

'What do you think was in the clearing?' she asked.

He shrugged. 'Who knows? Perhaps nothing except young girls' secrets.'

Sensing that he had disclosed all he would or could, Sophia spoke of other things, even Colin. Mr Gresham of course knew of the changes in her plans. 'We're very friendly still,' she assured him trying to sound offhand. 'I write to him almost every day. But perhaps we won't marry at all.'

As they neared the little path leading up the hill to

Roundstones she asked, 'Mr Gresham, when I last saw you I felt you wouldn't want to talk about the Tunnel Woods or Helen's diary. Why did you change your mind?'

'I thought Eleanor would have wanted it. And I've been thinking about you, Sophia, and whether you were made sad by the diary. I thought perhaps that's why you came back.'

He said goodbye, turned towards the footbridge but suddenly changed his mind, took her hand and kissed her cheek.

She stayed by the willow some time but gradually uneasiness made her hurry towards the house. She had recalled that Mrs Bubb's relentless gaze must often have followed her progress along the path by the river. And now she heard rustling behind her and Michael appeared.

'Oh for heaven's sake!' she exclaimed.

'I wondered when you'd like me to take you to the woods,' he said. 'I was there, remember.'

16

Only three weeks after the end of her previous visit Deborah Parditer returned to Needlewick. It was much too interesting there for her to stay away. How quickly events had moved: Eleanor's death, Sophia's visit, Colin, a broken engagement (for which Deborah took some credit having expressed doubts about the impending nuptials), and now Mrs Bubb with a stroke. Wretched woman, how like her to pick on an illness which would be as protracted and inconvenient to poor Margaret as possible. And to top it all Sophia had come back to Needlewick. Deborah was rewarded for years of intimacy with her Needlewick friends by being accepted into the fold without question at this time of trouble.

On the evening of her return she went to visit John Gresham, as was her habit, although such calls were an ordeal for both; she was confused by his grief and he fumbled for words or struggled to respond to her energetic suggestions for cheering himself up. But beneath the awkwardness was love, nurtured through years of afternoon calls, care of Eleanor and respect for differences.

He answered the door himself and ushered Deborah into the sitting-room where the evening sun poured across the furniture and revealed the smears on the window panes.

'Is that woman looking after you, John?' Deborah demanded, noting also the dust on the occasional table by the fire. 'Servants always take advantage of a single man.'

'I feel comfortable with her,' he said – not a satisfactory answer.

They drank sherry and discussed Mrs Bubb's illness.

'You're to stay well clear of that house, John. You've had enough of invalids,' said Deborah.

'I'm not needed there. You knew of course that Sophia has come back to help?'

He got up and went to the window, the sherry lapping dangerously in his glass.

'She's not much use, I'd have thought,' said Deborah. 'Probably she's here more for her own convenience than Margaret's. Still, at least she's a bit of young life. I don't suppose there's been any word from Helen?'

'I think not.'

'It seems so callous. Has the girl no feeling? Doesn't she remember how devoted Mrs Bubb was? I remember them so clearly together. You'd meet them in the post office, baby Helen clutching Mrs Bubb's skirts. Or you'd find them walking together in the lane.'

'Children quickly outgrow early affections.'

'Margaret never did,' Deborah said tartly. 'Margaret has stayed loyal to Mrs Bubb.'

Mr Gresham now took out a letter from his inside pocket. 'This came yesterday. I haven't mentioned it to anyone else yet. It's addressed to Eleanor, from Suzanna.'

'Surely not.' Deborah had to hold her curiosity firmly in check. The letter was inches from her hand. 'I assume you've read it?'

'Of course. I feel you should too. She wants to come back to Needlewick and asks Eleanor for support.'

Suzanna's handwriting was on the envelope, very small and untidy, the letters ill-formed, yet still familiar. Deborah had preserved all the scraps and notes she'd ever received from Suzanna.

'You'll need more light, it's difficult to read,' John said.

Switzerland
July 20, 1920

Dearest Eleanor,

I've been thinking about you more and more, what a long time since I wrote, since I saw you. How are you? Are you any better? I do think of you though I'm not much good to you, am I, or anyone, I sometimes think, not really here, I get so tired now. I wrap food and do the parcels for the refugees. Everyone is very patient but I keep thinking of Needlewick and how quiet it is there, not like here with all the people and foreign languages. I'm so tired, Eleanor, I work so hard and get nowhere, as usual.

How are you and what about dear John? Lucky Eleanor. I should have stayed in Needlewick, with the sun on the river, not come away. Sophia is not after all going to marry her great catch. Poor Sophia, what must she have gone through, I shall come at once and bring her with me to Needlewick − will Margaret be able to put us up, or could you if it's too much for her? A girl needs her mother and I will support her.

I wish someone had prevented me from marrying when I did but of course I was in love with Simon then and nothing could have stopped me marrying him.

And on the way home through France I shall visit Nicholas's grave. I've seen pictures of the cemetery – it looks so tidy don't you think, all those neat stones like dominoes, push one, and they'll all tumble down, one after another on to the grass. I wish you could have been there at Nicholas's service. I thought all the time if Eleanor had been here I could have held her hand. I needed you, Eleanor. The others came and kissed me but could do no good because they did not know my Nicholas. Nobody knew him as I did. I don't know how he could have been my son and so fine.

They are encouraging me to go home and will pay my fare because I have no money. I give all Simon's allowance to the Relief Fund because I know full well he would hate to know it went to foreign refugees and I would not touch it for myself, poison money.

Oh Eleanor, July in Needlewick, so green and quiet, and the sun on the river. Your garden will be lovely at this time of year I think and remember. Will John have his old white hat on while you are reading this? And later you will be washing raspberries and redcurrants and pressing them into a summer pudding. Shall we go for walks or are you still too unwell? Eleanor I'll sit with you and tell you about my adventures, poor little adventures, and bring you strength though I haven't much to give, which is perhaps why I'm writing at last because now I know how it feels to be so weak.

I'll come then, tell Margaret I'll write soon.

While Deborah read, John Gresham shuffled uneasily about the room, but came to rest near her chair and gazed tenderly into her face as he saw that she had reached the end. 'It's a sad letter, isn't it? She doesn't sound like Suzanna.'

Deborah spoke on an indrawn breath in a vain attempt to hold back tears. 'No, no, it doesn't sound like her at all. I thought she was so immersed in all that work. She was such a prominent figure during the war. Poor Simon, do you remember how hopping mad he was over those pacifist rallies?'

'Nicholas's death must have affected her very badly. It's only natural.'

'I was there at the service. She was very pale, I remember, and in a great hurry to get away. She seemed not to want to speak to anyone, least of all to Simon or Margaret or even Sophia.' Suzanna, she thought, I was there, I would have taken you in my arms; I knew how you loved your son. But you barely gave me a glance. As usual you did not want me.

'More sherry, Deborah?'

'Just a drop.'

'I thought, I must write and tell her again about Eleanor's death. And of course she can't stay at Round-stones with Mrs Bubb ill.'

'Jane will put her up,' Deborah offered, but there was an awkward pause as they both had a mental picture of Suzanna in Middlecote Hall taking tea with George Middlecote.

'Have you told Sophia about the letter?'

'I've not seen her since this came.'

'How is she?'

'Subdued.'

'She must be wondering what the future has in store for her. Really, that family seems to be doomed to unhappiness. What precipitated the end of her engagement?'

For an instant their eyes met.

They both knew.

17

The grim routine at Roundstones continued, a great strain even on Sophia because she stumbled along on the periphery, quite dispensable and therefore by no means absorbed by the drama.

She had developed devices for making her daily session in Mrs Bubb's room more bearable, and had established a way of speaking to the patient which satisfied her; polite and intimate, as if Mrs Bubb were indeed the cosy confidante she had never been in good health. Though Sophia imagined her words soaking through the housekeeper's skull to the red tissue of her brain and hushing and shushing their way into the woman's consciousness somehow, there was never any outward sign of response.

Having made the gesture of patting the bedclothes, Sophia settled herself at the window. 'I hope you don't mind but I've brought a letter from Colin to read. Amazingly enough he is still writing to me, despite the cruel way I ended our engagement. It makes me think sometimes that all that was a bad dream. I certainly enjoy his letters.'

Each time a letter arrived from London, Sophia opened it with the same jolt of anticipation. Would this be the love letter she at once longed for and dreaded? *Dearest Sophia, think again, I love you, I miss you, come back to me. I need you . . . !* Depending on her mood she responded to this imaginary letter either with a sad refusal or by ordering a taxi, speeding back to town and falling into his arms. Lying in her lonely bed at Round-stones, she often tried to visualise what it would be like to sleep next to Colin. She turned her head on the pillow and imagined him lying beside her, reached out and put a tentative hand on his hair.

But his letters were a terrible disappointment. Devoid of any mention of how he felt, they contained long amusing accounts of court cases or evenings with friends. Once he made an allusion to her father whom he had met for lunch. 'He is obviously very lonely and sorry about what has happened, but I'm afraid unrelenting towards you. I told him I thought you'd done the right thing and behaved quite properly but he would not be softened. He did say you were quite at liberty to return home.'

Sophia dwelt on this last sentence for some time, wondering if it was actually a concealed plea from Colin, but no, she thought, if he really wanted to see me he could always come to Needlewick. But then her reaction to his last surprise visit had scarcely been one of welcome and he would therefore probably not risk another rebuff. And she could not invite him to come because she mistrusted her feelings. She was afraid that, if she saw him, there would be a rebirth of the old irritation, and then she'd be trapped, because she could scarcely summon him to Needlewick simply to check that she still did not love him enough to marry him.

Once a letter was read and pondered over, it was time to check the prone figure on the bed. Was she wet or dirty or dry-lipped? No, quite all right. 'There you are, Mrs Bubb, you're all tidy.' Then Sophia would embark on a re-examination of the ornaments and photographs which by now she had studied intently. One, a copy of a print she had found tucked away in the nursery cupboard at home, was a stiff family group of her grandparents and two small girls; Margaret, serious and stolid, and Suzanna, slight and, even in that faded picture, eye-catching with her light hair and the suggestion of a naughty smile. Another photograph was taken in the garden at Roundstones, a family at tea on the lawn, so distant that Sophia could hardly make out her uncle and aunt with baby Helen. There were two wedding photographs (Suzanna and Simon Theobald, and Harry and Margaret Callwood) and one of Helen, perhaps a year or two younger than she had been during Sophia's first Needlewick summer, standing alone in the garden with her startled eyes shadowed by a big hat. There was one more picture, so blurred that Sophia wondered why it had been thought worth retaining, of two girls, probably Suzanna and Margaret, perhaps on the lawn at Round-stones. They stood in middle distance on grass but their forms were so indistinct they were scarcely recognisable. There were no mementoes of Mr Bubb, nor indeed any indications that Mrs Bubb had a family of her own at all.

On the afternoon following her walk with Mr Gresham Sophia asked, 'I wonder if you can tell me anything about the Tunnel Woods, Mrs Bubb? I went that way yesterday.'

She moved her chair closer to the bed. The patient's face was turned aside and her eyes were closed.

'You know Helen took me there. You must have seen us on that path many a time.'

The room's silence was intensified by the cacophony of birdsong outside. 'And then of course my mother went there often, Mr Gresham said. Were *you* ever in the Tunnel Woods?'

Sophia placed her hand on Mrs Bubb's cheek to turn her face and stroked the warm forehead fiercely in an attempt to open the eyes. 'What was there, Mrs Bubb? Do you know? Did they tell you?'

Finally she approached her mouth close to the old woman's ear. '*My people,*' she whispered, her own hair brushing the pillow.

And then, conscious of her proximity to the white linen sheets and the sick woman's half-open mouth, so close that the heat of exhaled breath reached her cheek, Sophia recoiled and moved to the window.

After a moment she said brightly: 'I'll read to you then, shall I?' She picked up Grimm and read aloud, failing to notice for several paragraphs that she had chosen the same story as the day before.

On Sunday, Sophia and her Aunt Margaret went to church. The building was full of resonance. In this very pew had sat her mother Suzanna and Margaret, and over there the Henshaw girls, making signals perhaps at Eleanor Carney, who was seated, demure and elegant between her parents. Sophia noticed that Deborah Parditer was back in Needlewick, alert as ever. And there was dear Mr Gresham – Sophia caught his eye and gave him a shy smile which he returned with a boyish grin. Sophia wondered what the vicar had been like in her mother's time; the current incumbent was a terrible bore and spoke at length on the theme of Bread in the Wilderness. She did not listen for long but instead speculated what secrets had been whispered in the porch after Communion services. Had her mother, sitting here on Sunday mornings, longed for the heavy Sabbath luncheon to be over so that she could hurry along the path to the Tunnel Woods? Today no such obstacle stood in Sophia's way because Sunday lunch, like every other midday meal at Round-stones these days, was cold. Nobody minded when Sophia said she would take a picnic and go for a walk.

To eat her lunch she sat on the same boulder in the river, made lonely by Mr Gresham's absence. She decided that she had never met anyone like him before. Such gentleness and kindness were rare. He would never judge her or dismiss her, whatever she did. He had looked so lonely and inconspicuous in the Gresham pew but Sophia wondered how the vicar dare preach so dry and un-imaginative a sermon to a man of Mr Gresham's intellect.

Her solitude was so oppressive that she was not quite as dismayed as usual to find herself watched by Michael. There he was, crouched on the bank, chewing a blade of grass.

'You've changed your mind then, I see,' he said.

'About what?'

'About going to them woods.'

'No, I haven't. I just thought I'd bring my lunch here to have a bit of peace and quiet.'

'Too noisy for you up at the house, is it?'

She did not rise to this sally but said, 'I expect you're

sorry about Mrs Bubb. You must have worked with her for years at Roundstones.'

Actually she had no idea whether he and Mrs Bubb ever spoke to each other in those days when he had worked for her uncle. She did not remember ever having seen him in the kitchen though he must have eaten there. Now she realised that she had angered him.

'The old sow's got what she deserved!' he said venomously. 'Always spying on people.'

Sophia was tempted to reply that this was a common fault among servants at Roundstones but said nothing.

'Are you coming then?' he demanded.

Sophia found that the discussion of Mrs Bubb had somehow confused her. For a moment she and Michael had been on the same side and she did not feel as repulsed by him as usual. And she *was* eager to see the clearing again.

'Are you sure you can get into the woods?' she asked.

'I go there often.' He reached out his hand to help her off the boulder. 'Come on then. It won't take long.'

Ignoring his proffered help, she jumped back on to the path and walked towards the Tunnel Woods, frightened, in a nervous, anticipatory way but more of being disappointed than by the nature of her companion. The gusty breeze and warm air sapped her energy; she felt too lethargic to resist. Besides the Tunnel Woods were an irresistible lure.

They scarcely spoke. Michael soon overtook her but halted occasionally to check her progress. His gait was jerky, hurried.

'How often do you go the woods?' she asked.

'Often. Good poaching territory.'

'You remember the clearing where you surprised Helen and me?' she asked reluctantly. She had to be sure.

'Oh yes.'

'I suppose you often followed us there.'

He did not reply but it seemed unlikely that he was silent out of shame. She noticed that he was panting and, wondering if he was perhaps asthmatic, she called: 'Do you want to slow down?'

He stopped so abruptly that she walked into him. Pushing her gently away he said, 'I'm all right.'

The unexpected physical contact had been unnerving. Sophia's fear of him was no longer suppressed by excitement at the prospect of seeing the clearing again – she had just collided with the body of a muscular, full-grown man, not the rather puny boy of her memory.

After a moment she said: 'I think it might be a little too far for me today. Perhaps another time. I have to look after Mrs Bubb.'

'We're nearly there. See!'

And indeed they were very near the closed entrance to the woods. 'Yes, so we are,' she said. 'I'll perhaps see how you get in but I don't think I'll go all the way to the clearing today.'

When they reached the woods he turned away from the river and walked along by the fence. Then, where nettles and grasses seemed to grow strongest and tallest, he suddenly did a crab-like movement and disappeared from view. When Sophia reached the place she found him holding brambles aside for her. Behind him a little square of fence had been cut carefully away. Once they were through Michael moved confidently among the dark trees. She followed cautiously, wary of tearing her stockings, and found to her relief that they soon reached a well-marked path.

'Is this the way to the tunnels?'

'Clever, aren't I?'

As they walked she searched for familiar landmarks but remembered no individual tree or twist in the way. Overhead the sky was now completely overcast and the woods were dim and dusty. She had forgotten how steeply the path climbed away from the river and how narrow it was in places. But she had not forgotten the tunnels.

They came upon the entrance so suddenly that Sophia had no warning until she realised that Michael had stopped and was waiting for her. 'Here we are,' he said.

To play for time she said, 'I'll get my breath back before I go on. It's quite a climb, isn't it?' She could not imagine why she had come so far with him. All she knew was that it would be impossible for her to plunge into the darkness beside him. It had been bad enough with Helen holding her hand, and even then . . . Sophia remembered that terrible game they had played on the last visit when she had been left to stumble alone down the echoing tunnel.

'I've often thought there must be a way over the top,' she said conversationally. 'I remember Helen once said these tunnels were only built as follies.'

'You can get over the top. How do you think I managed not to be seen when I followed you?' He brought his face up close to hers. 'There's nothing to be afraid of.

These woods are quite ordinary. Not even that big. I know them well.'

The skin on his nose was large-pored. She could smell his sweat and his breath, surprisingly sweet.

'Let's go over the top then,' she said.

'That would take far too long.'

'It would be much more interesting for me. I've only ever been through the tunnels.'

'As I remember, you were always pretty afraid of them.'

He'd seen it all then.

'I'm glad I didn't know at the time that you were watching us,' she said.

'Come on. I'll hold your hand. You'll be all right.'

'I'm sorry, Michael. I'm tired. I've had enough. Some other time. I must get back to Mrs Bubb.'

'You've got plenty of time. Come on.'

Too late she realised the extent of her danger because when she turned away he clasped her wrist with his thin, strong fingers.

'Michael,' her voice quavered and pleaded.

'Come on, you little bitch. Come and see the tunnels. Come with me.'

She tried to wrench her hand free but he changed his grip to her upper arm and then swung her round to hold her fast by gripping her waist with both hands. 'Frightened, are you? Scared of little Michael, the doctor's boy?' He was backing into the tunnel. 'Frightened of a poor boy who dared to give you cheap scent.'

'What do you mean?' The darkness was closing around her.

'You threw it away. I found it in the hedge. It cost me a lot, the ticket that won me that.'

'I was only a child. I'm sorry.'

'Only a child, yeah. Are you still a child? With your dainty little shoes and silky clothes?'

He twisted her back against the tunnel wall. Its unyielding dampness was almost a relief; at least it was solid.

'All right,' he said 'We won't go to the clearing. We'll stop here and have a bit of fun. You haven't had much of that, have you?'

It was very dark. She could scarcely see him at all, only, very dimly, his eyes. And it occurred to her that he was an expert at this game; she could imagine him ripping screaming rabbits from snares. His hands were expert hands. One hand he moved from her waist to her neck, forcing her head back and up so she could no longer speak without pain. Then he pushed his knee between her legs and his body hard up against hers. Although she could move her hands she was weakened and pinioned by his hold on her neck.

'What shall we do then, eh? Talk together like you and that gentleman friend? You liked talking to him, didn't you? Didn't get much else done did you? Poor chap. I felt quite sorry for him. It never pays to be too much the gentleman, does it?'

Had she been able to speak she would not have screamed or pleaded with him to release her. A question had suddenly dropped clear and demanding into her head and was awaiting an opportunity. *What else did you see in the clearing?* is what she would have asked. But the pressure of his hand on her neck had made her faint and she was supported only by the forward thrust of his body.

The blackness of the tunnel came inside her head. His voice was very distant. 'I preferred you when you used to have your hair loose on your shoulders. It swayed in time to the hem of your dress.' He pulled at her hair with his free hand. Pins dropped down the neck of her blouse. 'Lovely hair. I remember your hair. You used to push it back, like this, and flick it from your shoulders. It was your way of showing it off. I touched it once as you hurried away from me. You'd never speak to me, would you?'

He stroked her hair gently, rubbing it between finger and thumb, then ran his fingers across her face.

'I watched when you sat in the field by the river, you and her. I watched your mouth, always opening and shutting, telling her tales. Sometimes you smiled and I wanted you to smile at me but you never did, not properly, only laughing at me.'

His fingers probing the skin near her nose smelt of the woods, of green things he'd pushed aside. His finger tips were hard but his touch was gentle.

'All I had of you was the odd glimpse of your petticoat, or the flick of your hair in my face. But when you went away I remembered the smell of you. I dreamt about you coming back and me getting you like this, here, you see, where you couldn't escape. So I could show you.'

He was caressing her lips, teeth and chin.

The pressure of his hand on her neck was released a little as he moved his fingers from her mouth to join his other hand at her throat, holding her neck quite softly in his two hands. Then he leaned forward and put his lips to her ear. 'You could have bitten me, I gave you the chance to get away.'

His taut body moved against hers in a spasm of excitement and fear.

'You won't forget me again, little bitch. You've stayed in my head. I've waited for you. Well I'll make you remember me. I will.' He was breathing so hard that when he moved his lips through her hair and across her cheek to her mouth his kiss was interrupted by his need to gasp for air. When he kissed her, his breath was sweet and soft. Her mouth fell open in surprise and his tongue darted against her teeth, the roof of her mouth and back across her lips. His hand moved from her neck to her breast; with finger and thumb he stroked it softly, felt for the nipple and squeezed, then his fingers edged across her stomach before unexpectedly cupping her hard between her legs. Her head shot back and his mouth fell on her chin. For an instant she listened to the pulsing of her body, then, sensing his distraction, pulled away from his warm hands and ran.

She stumbled out of the tunnel and down to the river where the newly erected barrier no longer posed a problem; she simply plunged knee deep into the water and waded along by the bank until she could climb back on to the path. On she ran, feet soaked and her wet dress heavy about her legs. All the time she cried, not for herself but for Michael whom she had treated with contempt one last, shameful time. Knowing her strength she had laid the bait, allowed him to give her a paltry measure of excitement, and then run. And all for one wet-lipped kiss and the grip of strong hands in a dark tunnel.

At Roundstones she met Susan Makepeace in the kitchen passage who told her that Mrs Bubb had taken a sudden turn for the worse; 'and that Mr Gresham was asking for you.'

'When was he here?'

'A few moments ago. I've just shown him out.'

Sophia hurried along the hall and out of the front door. 'Mr Gresham!'

He was not in sight but she ran along the lane and caught up with him near the gate. 'Mr Gresham!' When he turned to face her, she realised how extraordinary she must look with her hair tangled down her back and her dress drying in muddy creases around her calves. She stopped short.

'I just got back. I heard you called.'

For a moment she was caught off balance because it occurred to her that Mr Gresham was probably, at that moment, more dear to her than anyone else and that she had run after him out of a blind desire for comfort, even absolution for what had happened with Michael in the tunnel. She longed to weep on his shoulder. Instead, they stood at the gate, side by side.

'I was so sorry to learn about Mrs Bubb,' he said. 'I would not have called had I known she was so ill.'

'What happened? I didn't stop to ask.'

'A second stroke, I believe, about an hour ago.'

Each had a hand on the rough wood of the gate. The field beyond sloped upwards in tufts and hillocks,

trampled and pitted by cows which now clustered together under trees in a far corner. Early evening in
August, and the sun was already casting deep shadows.

'I brought you this.' He handed her Suzanna's letter.
Her hands trembled as she unfolded the paper but she
read steadily and without obvious emotion.

'This must have been hard for you to read,' she said
afterwards. 'I can't understand why she thinks Mrs
Gresham is still alive. Surely she was told.'

'She seems confused, don't you think?' he said gently.

'Her letters are always muddled, the few I've had, a
great jumble of ideas and experiences.'

'And it's very hard to read her writing which used to be
so clear,' he added. 'I showed this to Deborah Parditer.
We both think your mother seems ill and distressed. I
think you should not therefore rely on her coming,
Sophia. And if she does come here she may not be quite
as you remember her.'

'I know I can't depend on her.' She was ashamed of the
tremor of self-pity in her voice. 'Well, thank you for
showing it to me.'

'I think we can do nothing until we know what her
intentions really are.'

'No.'

It seemed to Sophia that the backwater of Needlewick
had, that afternoon, contained so much drama and emotion she would never recover. She shrank from the
memory of what had happened in the tunnel and wished
that this moment with Mr Gresham, watching the
tranquil cows in the late sunlight, could expand until it
was all that was left.

She sighed, glanced at him, and saw that he was absorbed by the stillness of the evening, half-smiling. Perhaps it was enough to know that he too was content at that moment.

She said: 'I should go. I may be needed back at the house.'

He shifted his hand very slightly so that his little finger brushed hers. 'Goodnight, then, Sophia.'

She was aware, as she walked away, that he was watching her, and the knowledge gave her the courage to re-enter the house.

18

Watching over Mrs Bubb was now much more of an ordeal. There was no question of reading Grimm; it seemed to Sophia that it would have been irreverent to pour fantasy into the ear of one so close to death. Mrs Bubb was apparently now completely unconscious, her eyes were always closed and the blood had drained from her face and hands leaving the skin a yellowish grey. Sophia took books and sewing up with her, but found she could do nothing but watch minute by minute for the moment of death. The suspense was nerve-racking.

Outside the sickroom the house was running more smoothly. Aunt Margaret had resigned herself to the loss of Mrs Bubb and had begun to pick up the threads of the household. Susan Makepeace was a sulky but quite intelligent girl. She would perform all her allotted tasks and then sit in the kitchen with her hands folded, waiting until told to do something else. Once she was found to be dependable enough to arrive on time in the morning, it had been decided that she could live out, and each evening at eight she hurried back down the hill to the village. Sophia had never made her intended visit to Mrs Makepeace. She felt exposed by the fact that Susan cleaned her room and washed her clothes; those big Makepeace eyes missed nothing. But her aunt seemed pleased with Susan who was malleable and willing compared to the stubborn Mrs Bubb.

The trickle of calls had ebbed a little as Mrs Bubb's condition stabilised, but they gradually increased in volume as news spread of her relapse. But no-one came to see Mrs Bubb, all were Margaret's friends who acted almost as if she were dying too – or as if she needed tending like a fragile flower whose prop is about to be torn away. Sophia didn't believe Aunt Margaret was fragile and was impatient with answering sorrowful questions.

Deborah Parditer called. Knowing the Roundstones routine as well as the inhabitants themselves, she came when the nurse was resting and Margaret with the patient because she wanted to speak to Sophia. The afternoon was fine and they sat on the terrace where Sophia felt less intimidated by her visitor. Susan served them tea; she had become expert at setting the tray and cutting thin bread and butter.

Mrs Parditer said officiously, 'You're poor Mrs Bubb's replacement, are you, dear? What's your name?'

'Susan Makepeace, madam.'

'Ah, a Makepeace girl. Well, I'm told you're doing well. And you're very lucky to have found such a good position with dear Mrs Callwood. How is your poor mother?'

'All right thank you.'

Susan retreated to count her blessings leaving Sophia alone with the inquisitor.

'It's such a pity about the garden,' said Deborah Parditer, 'it's amazing how everything seems to slip when there's sickness.'

'The garden always seems lovely to me.'

'I expect you're not used to much by way of gardens in London.' She paused for a moment, and then said: 'I expect John showed you the letter from your mother.'

'Yes.'

'You've heard nothing else from her?'

'Not a word.'

'I don't envy your uncertainty but I expect you're used to your mother's little ways.'

'They don't affect me much. I've scarcely seen her since she left home years ago.'

Mrs Parditer sat back in her chair and eyed Sophia curiously. 'I admire your mother, Sophia. She has so much courage. She has always gone her own way and tried to do right. Her life since leaving your father can scarcely have been easy.'

'Most people say she was foolish and unwomanly to give up her family to work for the suffrage.'

'Leaving your father did seem very rash at the time. But I remember when I heard about it I wasn't surprised. No, I seem to have expected it. Your mother was never one to be tied down. Even as a girl Suzanna was always off on one wild scheme or another.'

'But you can't have expected her to leave my father and me. Surely no-one could have foretold such a thing.'

'We all thought it romantic when your father came and swept her off her feet like that. You can imagine how we girls used to sit up late at night gossiping and speculating. We had nothing better to do. The whole district was agog with it – the romance of the rich Londoner and the local doctor's daughter.'

Sophia sat up suddenly realising that in Deborah

Parditer she had found a fertile source of information. She poured more tea, cut more cake, and asked casually: 'How did they meet?'

'By chance. He was looking over some land with a view to purchase. And after that he wouldn't leave her alone. He called or wrote daily until she had agreed to marry him.'

'He's never recovered from her leaving.'

'Hasn't he been tempted to marry again?'

'They were never actually divorced.'

'And he wasn't a man ever to sympathise with her cause,' said Deborah, 'so it was a double blow. She couldn't have chosen anything more wounding to him. He was the very last sort of man ever to condone the idea of women having power.'

'What about the rest of you here, what did you think?'

Deborah was pleased to give her opinion. 'Those women did some pretty extraordinary things – your own mother – sticking safety pins in tyres – so extreme and wild and sordid, I used to think. The idea of ladies in prison! And then in the war she did all that marching for peace and tried to stay friendly with the German women. We couldn't accept that, we were terribly patriotic, of course, and hated the pacifists. I couldn't understand Suzanna going along with all that; she had always been so strong-willed and clear-minded but I decided that she must have been indoctrinated. However, lately, I've begun to feel she might, after all, have been right.' Mrs Parditer had finished her tea. 'Shall we stroll down to the river before I go up to see Margaret?'

She picked up her capacious bag and they walked slowly across the lawn, Deborah pausing occasionally to point out some flaw in the border. 'Yellow roses are always a mistake. They look blown and faded almost before they're fully out . . . I'm surprised at your aunt for allowing the mignonette, it's such an untidy plant.'

Sophia unlatched the garden door for her and they stood looking out over the valley towards Middlecote Hall.

'And what about you, Sophia, what are you going to do with yourself?'

'I don't know. I'm needed here.'

'Your aunt could manage perfectly well without you. She's very efficient, although she must be feeling that woman's loss pretty badly. It's always a mistake to be too dependent on one person.'

'How do you mean dependent? Isn't one always dependent on one's servants?'

'My dear, from the moment Mrs Bubb arrived, the entire family relied on her to a ridiculous extent. Your grandmother was hopeless, she simply couldn't be a mother to Margaret and Suzanna. She managed to produce them, but that was it. She could never settle, never focus on them properly. The poor things would have been terribly neglected were it not for Mrs Bubb.'

'I could never warm to Mrs Bubb when I was a child. She seemed to hate me.'

'She would. You weren't at all like Suzanna, you see.'

'My father accuses me of being just like her,' Sophia said, suddenly in need of comfort.

'There is much to admire in Suzanna. But of course she lacks stability.'

Sophia's heart was beating very fast. For once she did

not try to defend her mother, but asked: 'Why do you think she and Aunt Margaret are so different?'

Mrs Parditer took Sophia's arm and leaned on her heavily as they walked down to the river. 'Poor Margaret, she was younger, plainer and she played safe. Mrs Bubb sheltered her by keeping her at Roundstones more. But Mrs Bubb would not or could not hold Suzanna. Young girls are vulnerable, Sophia, easily influenced. Your mother had a very odd few years here in Needlewick before she married your father. She became isolated and took to rambling about all over the place by herself. I'm afraid we all – except Margaret – rather gave up on her in the end. So in some ways it was a very good thing your father turned up.'

'Why do you think she was like that, though?'

'I've no doubt you've heard plenty of gossip. There were wheels within wheels. Fanciful girls. I kept my own daughters under a very tight rein. In that way, of course, Suzanna is right to do all her shouting and running about demanding decent education and responsibility for women. Girls need to have their heads filled with know-ledge the same as boys, otherwise they pack their own heads with all kinds of nonsense. What nonsense is your head filled with?'

'None, I hope.' But Sophia could not help blushing as she thought of her shameful treatment of first Colin, then Michael.

'We'll go on the bridge,' Deborah announced. 'Why did you finish your engagement to young Kilbride? Nice chap, I thought.'

Though startled by the directness of the question

Sophia found herself answering: 'I suppose I don't love him.'

'That's reason enough. You don't want to make the same mistake as your mother.'

'But she loved my father.'

'Yes. She was desperately in love at first. But she was also completely enchanted by the world he offered her – the escape from Needlewick.'

'But you said she was so happy here. You said she loved the countryside.'

'Did I say she was happy? And she didn't *love* it here. She was mesmerised. Haven't you ever wanted to join any of your mother's causes?' Mrs Parditer was not to be distracted from her main line of enquiry.

'It has occurred to me, just recently, that I might write to Mother about it. But I don't feel very passionately about anything.'

Mrs Parditer sighed and turned restlessly away. 'Yes, you're a typical product of our age; a bright girl with nothing to do and no skill but an eye for a well-cut frock or a handsome man, and suddenly you find neither is enough. We were lucky, you see. We never expected anything else, but women like your mother have destroyed all that. Women will never have peace of mind again. They won't knuckle under. You're sure about Kilbride?'

'Oh heaven knows!' Sophia said irritably.

'If I were you I'd find myself an alternative occupation fast or you'll go and do the wrong thing out of sheer desperation. But don't go overboard like your wretched cousin. She's another one who's got very strange.'

Mrs Parditer turned back towards the house and walked more swiftly up the path.

Sophia, seeing her chance slip away, called: 'Do you remember the Tunnel Woods? What happened there? Tell me, please!'

Deborah paused but did not turn to look at Sophia. 'I never knew and now I don't think it much matters. Yes, we went along the tunnels, and we found a clearing, a lovely place, very quiet, almost circular. And Suzanna said afterwards she had to go back. I don't know why. She would never let anyone except Margaret go with her. At first we asked them about their visits, but neither would give any details. I know that Margaret was always instructed to wait outside the tunnels. I used to think of her there, waiting for Suzanna. I never liked those woods. We thought Suzanna was being very selfish and childish. Why do you ask?'

'I went with Helen. And I'd love to go back, just to see.' Sophia, distracted by the memory of her own last visit to the woods, faltered. 'I've walked that way but it's all fenced up. Did you know? I can't imagine why anyone would want to do that.'

Mrs Parditer was now waiting by the wall, watching her. 'Surely you've been told?'

'No. I just think, how odd of the owner to go to all that expense.'

Mrs Parditer's hand was on the latch of the garden door. She stared at Sophia in astonishment. 'But surely you know who those woods belong to now? Your father bought them as a wedding present for your mother.'

19

Mrs Bubb died in the early hours of a late August morning. After all the waiting, it was strange to find that nothing much had changed; there was only a general sigh of relief that she had at last gone. For that day at least Sophia could be properly helpful by writing notes and discussing arrangements for the funeral. She did not go up to see the body but was deeply troubled by its presence in the house. When she went to rest in her room after lunch she could think of nothing but the corpse upstairs and the way Mrs Bubb's slippers had lain slightly crooked under the washstand for so long, waiting for their owner to shuffle into them. When she got up and looked out into the garden she imagined Mrs Bubb staring at the same view day after day, year after year.

In the afternoon a few flowers came but of course none from any of Mrs Bubb's relatives.

'Did she have no family at all?' Sophia asked.

'There was her husband, of course,' said Aunt Margaret. 'They had a house in the village when she first worked here. He died before they had any children. Consumption, I think. But she belonged here at Roundstones.'

Aunt Margaret seemed to have accepted the death calmly, but several times in the afternoon Sophia heard her go upstairs to Mrs Bubb's room. Margaret looked dreadful in black. When Sophia suggested that in the case of Mrs Bubb mourning need not be worn she was sharply rebuked. 'Sophia! She was my very dear companion. I owe her so much more than this.'

'You were very good to her. She was fortunate to have such a comfortable home.'

'No, Sophia, it was she who provided a home for me.'

By the evening all arrangements had been made and the proper people notified, including Helen who responded to her mother's telephone call by saying she would come at once. The day of the funeral was fixed – and beyond that, for Sophia, was a terrible blank. Her uncle said that he would like a holiday. Soon Roundstones would be empty.

After dinner Sophia took the path down to the river. The sun was setting behind a thick bank of cloud, the sky above was a faded golden blue and all the trees on the opposite side of the valley were etched darkly into the hillside. There was no light on the river, only shadow. The branches of the willow hung quite still.

She had not walked towards the Tunnel Woods since that shameful time with Michael and did not now, though she no longer feared him. She had not seen him since that day but sensed that he would not attempt to touch her again. Instead she planned to walk over the footbridge and up the field path to the church. She was tempted to call on Mr Gresham but, on reflection, decided such an action was out of the question. She dared not approach him in the quiet of the evening with

Mrs Bubb dead and the sun setting over Needlewick. Such an act would be too significant, too laden with a craving for companionship. She loved Mr Gresham far too much to risk hurting him in that way.

At the bridge she stopped dead. A woman wearing a long brown coat and heavy hat and carrying a clumsy bag was walking down the field towards her. Sophia recognised her at once but was unable to form a word of greeting.

'Sophia, is it you?'

Suzanna put her bag down on the bridge in order to embrace her daughter, who was hurtled back to childhood by that faint, familiar perfume which assailed her the instant their cheeks touched – her mother in a rustling pale gown kissing her goodbye before departing for the opera or a reception.

Sophia held her close. 'I didn't expect you.'

'I got your letter. I wanted to be home. How's Mrs Bubb?'

Was that all she cared about? 'I'm afraid she died this morning. I'm awfully sorry.'

Suzanna held on to the wooden rail of the bridge and gazed upstream. 'It's so long since I was here. Perhaps even before you were born.'

Overhead white streaks of cloud swam over the blue. A bird sang clear and cool-throated from a tree by the river and the water flowed quietly. Suzanna stood quite still, watching. Sophia noticed that the sleeve of her coat, too heavy for a summer evening, was very worn. 'Have you come far today?' she asked softly, and then as Suzanna turned dreamily towards her exclaimed: 'Oh you look so tired!'

'Yes, I am tired. I need a little rest. Or so they told me. How's Mrs Bubb?'

'She died this morning.'

'I thought she would die. She must have been very old. And what about you, Sophia? I was surprised that you came here. I didn't think you'd like it in Needlewick. You didn't last time you came, do you remember, when you were a girl? You wrote all those letters to me, so brave, such a brave little girl but I knew you were hating it.'

'I like it now. It's peaceful.'

'Yes, it's peaceful here though terribly poor still. I must go to the cottages in the morning. I thought it would be all right to come back; I need a holiday. I haven't had a holiday for such a long time, not since Nicholas died really.'

'Shall we go up to the house, Mother? Aunt Margaret will be very pleased to see you.'

'I ought to have written, she never used to like surprises. But I didn't have time. They thought I should have a little rest. But it's not really fair on Margaret, she's got enough on her plate. How's Mrs Bubb?'

Sophia was so afraid that she could scarcely bring herself to pick up Suzanna's bag and draw her away from the river. This woman was so terribly unlike her bright, quick, beautiful mother. Instead she was vague, nervy, her movements fumbling, like a sleepwalker's. Why does she not listen to my answers? Sophia thought. Why did she not show more emotion at seeing me?

Suzanna paused several times on their way up the hill and turned to look back over the valley.

'It's peaceful here,' she murmured, 'so still. I should have come back before.'

'I find it restful after London.'

'I never really liked London though I thought I would because I was glad to escape from here. But this is where I belong.'

The open french windows and lit drawing-room were a relief after the dark garden and Sophia thought that perhaps the brightness would restore her mother to normality.

But Suzanna stood blinking at the window. 'Nothing changed,' she said.

'Oh, it must have done. Aunt Margaret said she had new loose covers only a couple of years back. You sit down here, mother, and I'll make tea and fetch Aunt Margaret.'

Suzanna would not sit but moved about the room. It struck Sophia suddenly that only her mother's slender ankles were unchanged – they at least were still elegant.

She went in search of her uncle whom she met on the stairs. As Sophia told him about her mother a mantle of professionalism descended on Harry – his initial shock at the news of Suzanna was replaced by reassurance. 'Yes, make some tea, Sophia, your aunt is resting in her room. I don't want her disturbed. I'll look after your mother.'

When Sophia returned to the drawing-room Harry and Suzanna were seated by the empty fireplace. He had taken Suzanna's coat which lay in an ugly heap on the sofa. She looked a little more herself, but dreadfully thin in a loose-fitting fawn dress and bowed down by her huge, hideous hat. Sophia wondered how her mother could wear such dreary clothes.

When Sophia came in, Suzanna sat bolt upright and smiled brightly, a gesture which caused Sophia a stab of pain. Were they such strangers that her mother must correct her posture and expression in this way?

'Your mother's come all the way from Switzerland. She's been doing great work there,' Harry said.

'What, Mother?'

Suzanna looked nervously at her daughter. After all, Sophia thought, I have no right to ask, she has received nothing but indifference from me.

'Mostly for the women and children, poor things. So much needs to be done. There were so many refugees.' Suzanna gripped the arms of her chair as if determined to get up and return to work.

Harry placed a tea cup in her hands. 'You are hungry, I expect. Your daughter here has become quite an expert in the kitchen over the past few weeks. What shall she make for you?'

'I've done nothing but eat. You know what journeys are like!'

'We have lovely fresh eggs,' Sophia said stupidly. It seemed imperative to feed this fragile creature.

But the idea of food seemed to sicken Suzanna.

'You go and make up the bed in Helen's room,' Harry suggested to Sophia. 'It used to be your old room didn't it, Suzanna? You'll be able to have a good sleep there.'

'Oh no, I came to look after Mrs Bubb. She used to be very good to us when we were children, she was so kind to me. I thought I must come and lend a hand to make her better.'

'Mrs Bubb died this morning,' Harry said, 'so we'll all be glad of an uninterrupted night's sleep.'

'I told you, Mother,' Sophia said reproachfully.

'Don't you think she's grown like her father, Harry?' Suzanna asked suddenly. 'Nicholas always took after me. I went to France, you know, to see where he died. But I couldn't find the exact place. It was raining.'

Sophia went to Helen's room and made the bed, opened the window to admit the night air, tiptoed out to the garden and gathered a few roses to place on the dressing-table. She heard her uncle go to the bedroom and talk to Margaret; together they went down to the drawing-room and closed the door.

Sophia was bitterly disappointed. During the last weeks she had conceived vague plans of reconciliation. Her mother had even become a symbol of possible redemption. She thought she would embrace one of her mother's causes and perhaps find a niche for herself. But it had become painfully clear, even from those brief moments in the drawing-room, that Suzanna was in some ways a refugee herself, with all her strength and passion subdued. There remained only a kind of hectic desire not to be a nuisance.

Sophia went into the kitchen, prepared a tray with cheese, fruit and cake, and carried it into the drawing-room, but even as she opened the door she realised the hopelessness of this activity; her mother was lying back in the chair, sobbing helplessly.

Margaret and Harry escorted Suzanna up to bed while

Sophia tidied the room and sat down to eat the supper, a ritual she could not afterwards understand.

Harry came back.

'Is she very sick?' Sophia asked.

'It's hard to say. We'll be able to tell more in the morning. She'll sleep now. So should you.' He led her to the foot of the stairs where she kissed him and went slowly up to bed.

20

Helen turned up the next morning wearing a surprisingly smart blue dress and navy hat – her glasses winked in the sunlight as she stood in the porch. The prodigal was returned. Margaret's pleasure and nervous deference were painful to watch. Anxious not to intrude on a Callwood family reunion, Sophia retreated to her own mother's room.

Suzanna had slept well and now lay quietly in Helen's narrow bed, staring at the open window through which she could see the cheerful, wind-puffed clouds. Beside her bed was a photograph – one that had previously been in Mrs Bubb's room – of two indeterminate figures under a tree. Suzanna looked very peaceful, mercifully unaware that Harry had contacted Simon Theobald.

'He must know that his wife is here and in a poor state of health,' he told Sophia firmly. 'He has a duty to support her and a right to be told where she is.'

'Uncle, she won't see him. And if she does he'll frighten her and make her even more unhappy.'

'I won't suggest he comes to Needlewick and I certainly wouldn't let him see her if I thought he wouldn't be gentle with her.'

But when told by telephone that Suzanna was in

Needlewick, Theobald said that he would cancel all engagements and motor down immediately.

Sophia was amazed by this concern, and very worried. The last time she had seen them together was Nicholas's funeral when she had watched them carefully, hoping for reconciliation in that moment of shared grief. Their eyes had met once, and Suzanna had walked towards him with extended hands. Theobald had waited until she was very close before turning away.

Sophia took an action she would not otherwise have considered; she telephoned Colin and asked him to come with her father. 'He won't understand the state she's in,' she told Colin desperately. 'I just don't know what will happen when they meet. He needs someone who'll be on his side.' Colin replied calmly that he would ensure that her father did not come to Needlewick alone and added that he was convinced the meeting would be very civilised.

When she had replaced the receiver, Sophia found that her hands were shaking and her heart pounding. Why had she involved Colin? What had she brought on herself?

Her mother seemed pleased to see her that morning. When Suzanna smiled the years melted away – her teeth were a little discoloured, her skin had lost its gloss and her eyes their brightness but the shape and enchantment of her smile were the same. She wanted to know the cause of the commotion downstairs but lost interest when she heard Helen had arrived. 'I don't think I've ever met her, have I? Perhaps at Nicholas's service. I don't remember. Wasn't she a rather plain little thing?'

'Very clever. She's at university.'

'It's odd, isn't it – I used to think my children would shine and poor Margaret's daughter would have no hope, confined to Needlewick as I had been. But Nicholas died. I never stop thinking of him, I imagine him all torn apart. He would have been such a great man, a kind man, not like your father.' The tears fell down her cheeks into her ears.

Sophia blurted out: 'Uncle Harry telephoned Father this morning and told him you were here. He said he'd come and see you.'

Suzanna did not seem troubled by this news after all. 'It'll be all right now I'm in Needlewick,' she said. 'Anyway, I'd like to see him, there's so much I need to discuss. We should have talked about your future much more carefully – and Nicholas's. If I'd had my way Nicholas would never have gone to war. It wasn't worth it, they should have listened to me.'

Sophia blotted her mother's tears. 'Nicholas had to go to the war, Mother, he was the right age. They needed him.'

'They didn't need him. My lovely boy! I loved him all those years and they gave him to German guns. It needn't have happened. They needn't have fought like that.'

'But, Mother, there had to be a war.'

'No, Sophia.' But Suzanna could sustain neither her anger nor her train of thought for long. She turned her head away. 'They wouldn't listen to us. But we were the women who gave birth to those boys for them. It costs a man nothing but a moment's pleasure to bring a child into the world. That's why life is so cheap to them. They don't pay and pay, body and soul.'

'Please, Mother, don't get too upset. Nicholas would hate you to cry for him like this.'

'Don't say that, Sophia. I asked too much of Nicholas – I always expected him to understand. He took too much on himself when he was only a child. Surely I can cry for him?'

'Oh Mother, I let you down so badly,' Sophia said bleakly, forgetting that Suzanna was ill and could give no comfort.

'You are your father's daughter, Sophia. You didn't let me down. You did exactly as I did. I chose your father. So did you.'

'I couldn't understand you. Nicholas always seemed to understand.'

'My lovely boy,' she cried, turning her head from side to side on the pillow. Then she recovered and took Sophia's hand. 'But I tell you what, Sophia, no-one can blame us for how we behaved. I won't let anyone reproach you.'

'What do you mean?'

'Neither of us had been taught to think. I had to have the truth hammered into me day by day, blow by blow, violently, because I didn't know how to learn. So I made so many mistakes and even now, sometimes, I forget everything and want only to come back here to Needle-wick. I'm so tired.'

'Will you go home to Father?'

'Never to your father.'

She was quiet for a while, then turned again towards the window and said softly: 'I met him here, you know.'

'Yes.'

'I thought, when I first knew him, that he would feel as I did about Needlewick. I used to take him everywhere; I showed him all my favourite places. He seemed so delighted. He was irresistible, Sophia. Well, you know that.'

Yes, Sophia knew her father's charm and power.

'But he took me away from Needlewick.' Her eyes strayed to the photograph by her bed. 'He took me away from the Tunnel Woods. There I am.' She looked at Sophia directly, as if for the first time. 'Sophia, we should have insisted on your receiving a proper education. It was so short-sighted. But I thought your looks and money would be enough. And you seemed bright.' She began to cry again and said weakly, over and over again, 'I wish you could have gone to a proper school.'

Sophia stroked her hair, and encouraged her to sleep. She was exhausted by her mother's emotion and helpless disappointment. Finally she murmured: 'It's not too late, mother. I'm not that old, I could still go to college.'

'You'll marry the man your father found you.'

'I told you I'm not engaged to him any more. Anyway, he's a good man.'

She was not listening. 'He's titled, isn't he? That would please your father.'

'Colin's been very generous to me.'

'That's what I thought about your father when he piled presents into my lap. Everything I could wish for, even the Tunnel Woods, as if that could ever bring them back to me.'

Sophia again wiped her mother's face and smoothed her hair. 'But you've led a good life, think of all those people you've helped. Father didn't take that away from you. Look at all you've done for those hungry people in Europe.'

But Suzanna was no longer listening.

Sophia found it strange to be in Roundstones with Helen again, and, despite herself, was amused to find that she now regarded Helen as the intruder, the disturber of the status quo. Suzanna had made little impact, sad and sick as she was – Roundstones seemed to have extended comforting arms to her and enclosed her effortlessly within its old walls. But Helen, who asked nothing at all, jarred the rhythm of the household. At lunch-time Sophia fancied that she could hear her cousin mentally drumming her fingers on the table at the tedium of the conversation. When it came to clearing the dishes between courses it was Sophia who leapt up to wait on Helen, anxious to protect her from the mundanities of life. The only topic that really attracted anything more than Helen's polite attention was that of Suzanna.

'Do you think I might go up and see her after lunch?' she asked. 'Just to introduce myself. I don't remember her at all, and I've always so admired her.'

'I suppose it can't do any harm,' her father said, 'but she's really not at all well, you must not excite her in any way.'

'I have a letter to post,' Sophia told Helen diffidently. 'I wondered if you'd come to the village with me later.'

'Yes, if you like.' Her indifference to Sophia was all the more galling because it was so clearly unaffected.

After lunch Helen disappeared upstairs while Susan Makepeace and Sophia washed up. 'It's a good job I'm here,' Sophia told Susan, 'otherwise you and poor Mrs Callwood would be terribly overworked. I don't think Helen is used to domestic life – she's got a very senior position at the university, you know.' Susan shrugged and slammed more crockery into the sink.

Later, when Sophia went upstairs, her mother's door was closed. From behind it she could hear women's voices.

By the time she and Helen left the house the sky had darkened and rain threatened.

'We'll have to walk quite quickly,' Sophia said. 'Are you sure you want to come? It may rain.'

'Oh yes, I don't get enough exercise these days, I'm sure.'

Conversation was tricky. Helen had no interest in small talk and made Sophia feel silly when she asked questions about her work. Sophia wished she could make some learned remark, which might impress or at least provoke discussion, but she was unable to produce anything.

'How long will you stay?' she asked tentatively.

'Lord knows. I don't expect I'll be able to stick it for long. Perhaps until Mother is ready to manage with the new Makepeace girl.'

It struck Sophia that Helen would in any case be of little use in helping her Mother over this difficult transition. 'Susan has made remarkable progress over the last few weeks,' she said.

'What about you? It's good of you to have stayed on so long. I expect you'll be wanting to go home.'

'I'll see what my father says. He'll be here soon. I'll obviously have to take care of mother.'

'I wouldn't worry. Mother seems quite happy to have adopted another invalid.' Helen's words contained no malice, yet Sophia felt dismissed, both from Needlewick and Suzanna's life.

'You went up to see her.'

'We had quite a little chat. She seemed all right, I thought.'

They were nearing the village.

'The place gets smaller every time I come back!' Helen said as they stood for a moment on the bridge at the foot of the High Street. 'The Makepeace place seems to be a little smarter.'

'I remember feeling such a grand lady when I visited Mrs Makepeace with you.'

'I suppose I did too, really. Shall we go in and say hello?'

'I don't think so. It's years since I was there. I've no reason to. You can if you like.'

Helen shook her head, obviously relieved, and hurried past the door.

'I'd like to call on Mr Gresham,' Sophia told her. 'He's been very kind to me since I've been here.'

'I wonder how you've put up with Needlewick, I really do. I couldn't, for any length of time.'

'Your mother seemed to need me.'

'Yes, there'll never be anyone like Mrs Bubb again. Poor soul!'

'Why do you say that?'

'She never had any life of her own, did she?'

'Don't you think so? She must have been happy at Roundstones. She had made herself part of it.'

'She was part of everything,' Helen replied sharply. 'Every part of my childhood. Every time I went out or came in, Mrs Bubb was there. She understood me better than anyone and knew if I had a sad or happy day.'

Sophia wondered why Helen had not rewarded such devotion by at least visiting Mrs Bubb during her last illness. Indeed Helen herself must have felt the need to justify this neglect because she added: 'I suppose I resented Mrs Bubb for knowing so much about me.'

They walked on in silence until they neared The Grey House where the sun emerged and shone hotly on the wall – they could smell the mortar. 'I hate it now Eleanor's dead,' Helen murmured.

Mr Gresham must have heard their approach because he was standing at the french windows.

'We won't disturb you!' Sophia called. 'Helen's here, and we've just been to the post office and thought we'd see if you were in.'

He took Helen's hand. It had been a mistake to come, Sophia could tell, but she had been unable to resist the chance to visit him.

'The garden looks as lovely as ever,' Helen said. Sophia thought that perhaps she was too short-sighted, even with her glasses, to see how overgrown it was, how weeds grew in the flowerbeds and the lawn needed cutting.

'I do my best,' Mr Gresham said.

'I'll come and give you a hand with it,' Helen offered

suddenly. 'I expect I'll be here for some days – until mother is settled with the new maid.'

He thanked her but seemed more alarmed than comforted by this suggestion.

They next spoke of Suzanna's sudden arrival.

Sophia said: 'I've come partly to say goodbye in case I don't get another chance. I may be leaving within the next couple of days depending on Mother.' No such plan had been formalised until that moment – it was this garden that had convinced Sophia that she had no further reason to stay in Needlewick. Sophia could do nothing to help Mr Gresham, who stood so uncertainly on the terrace – she could not offer to put his garden in order for him. 'So, if I don't see you again, goodbye, and thank you.'

They set off along the brick path where dandelions had pushed themselves up between the stones.

He called after Sophia: 'Did you ever get to the Tunnel Woods, then?'

She turned, very conscious of Helen. 'No, I never did. Goodbye, Mr Gresham.'

'He ought to move away,' Helen pronounced when they were at a safe distance from The Grey House. 'It's all too much for him now she's gone.'

'I don't think he could bear to leave Needlewick, do you?'

'Of course he could. It's foolish to brood on old memories of the past.'

Later Sophia said: 'Helen, my mother's in your room. Would you like me to put an extra bed in the guest room? I've been wondering where you might sleep.'

'Oh don't bother, I'll sleep on a sofa tonight. As soon as they move the body I'll use Mrs Bubb's room. I've always liked the view from up there.'

They could not pass Middlecote Hall without calling. Word would certainly have reached the family there of the new arrivals at Roundstones. It would be an unforgivable slight not to go in.

They were shown into the drawing-room where the sisters were at tea. Lady Middlecote at once leapt to her feet. 'My dear Helen, what a surprise! And Sophia!' They were embraced, ushered to the table and plied with tea and cake; attentions which had an unfortunate effect on Helen who withdrew into herself like a sea anemone.

'And how is Cambridge?' asked Lady Middlecote.

Helen said coldly, 'I'm not sure what you mean. My research is progressing well, thank you, especially as most of the students are on vacation. I still find the city an enjoyable place to live.'

'Your mother will be so pleased to see you. She misses you dreadfully, I know,' floundered poor Lady Middlecote.

'I think she's been rather occupied with Mrs Bubb,' said Sophia gently, 'and you know my mother has turned up?'

'Yes.' Mrs Parditer suddenly reached out and took her hand. 'How is your mother?'

'Very nervy, very unwell. Exhausted, I think. I'm afraid we are both rather a burden on poor Aunt Margaret at present.'

'Don't be silly, Sophia. She's probably delighted Suzanna's here. I told you that,' said Helen.

'And now my father is likely to appear at any moment,' Sophia added, 'and I'm afraid I'm rather dreading it.'

Mrs Parditer's interest, if possible, quickened. 'You think he'll come?'

'He's legally responsible for her, you see, so my uncle felt he should be told.' Sophia recognised that at last she had found someone who would understand her fears. 'I don't think Uncle Harry knows what my mother has endured, or how furious Father was when she left home. It won't be a happy meeting.'

Helen shifted uncomfortably in her chair. 'We've just called on Mr Gresham. He looks as if he's come to terms with his loss.'

Nobody quite knew how to respond to this remark.

21

They could see the glare of the sun on the bonnet of Colin's automobile even from the river and as Sophia laid her hand on the latch of the garden door at Roundstones she knew that she had reached a turning point; once inside she would be sucked into the whirlwind caused by the arrival of Colin and her father. Pulling down that stiff metal latch was one of the few actions in her life that she recognised as significant. And then the door was open, and there was no more time for reflection.

Colin was standing on the lawn with Aunt Margaret, waiting for her. When she took his hand, she could feel the warmth of his body though they did not kiss. His solidity was somehow a surprise after weeks during which she had been able to remember only the fall of his hair on his forehead or the way he had sat at table with father on the night her engagement to him had ended. Decide, she thought in a panic, even as she was welcoming him, whether you love him or not. You must decide.

They were left alone in the breezy garden. Her father was already closeted with Uncle Harry, and Margaret ushered away Helen to see about supper. Sophia took his arm and with the other hand held down her skirts, or pushed back long strands of hair fretted loose by the now considerable gusts of wind.

Colin did not seem nervous but looked about him with interest, telling her that she had written so much about Roundstones he could not fail to be curious on this second visit. He added that her father had seemed quite composed on the journey, although he had welcomed Colin as a travelling companion. They would both stay the night in Cheltenham where they had already booked rooms. Sophia was warmed by his air of competence; she had become so enmeshed in the dramas at Roundstones that his coming seemed to fling open the door of the outside world. She began to wonder whether the question of their future together would after all be raised immediately; she hoped not, she was so nearly sure but not quite.

But it became obvious that he was simply waiting for the right moment to speak because he paused, took her hand which had been resting on his arm and turned her to face him. 'I'm glad you telephoned me, Sophia, because I've been looking for an opportunity to speak to you again. I know that this is a particularly difficult time for you and I do not want to add to your troubles but yet I must speak.'

She had no premonition of what was to come; her mind was engaged only on what she would say, what would be her answer this time. She did not therefore see the pain in his eyes or interpret the sudden tightening of his fingers on hers.

'I've come to ask you to end our engagement once and for all,' he said.

She was so astonished that at first she couldn't speak. She thought stupidly, It is I who am doubtful, not him.

Then she said, without thinking: 'Does my father know this?'

They had walked to the part of the garden furthest from the house; an observer might have wondered at their sudden absorption in runner beans.

He did not attempt to hide his hurt or his contempt at her response but said at last: 'As a matter of fact, yes.'

'I'm sorry. That was a foolish question. It's not what I wanted to say.' She was very close to tears; the safety net which she had once made a feeble attempt to abandon but had actually retained to give her courage was now to be taken away then. She had no choice after all.

Colin continued: 'I think we both knew that once there was talk of postponement there could be no going back. One ought not to be ambivalent about whether or not to marry someone.'

'No.'

'I have felt the strain of indecision. I want to be free of you completely. I can't go on like this.'

She could not resist asking: 'Is there someone else then?'

They had wandered on and were now by the garden door. He leant upon it and the sun, making a brief appearance through a torn gap in the clouds, shone full on him. 'You still don't understand how much I loved you, do you, or you wouldn't ask that? I just won't subject myself to any more pain.'

She laid her head against his shoulder, so that her cheek was turned to the warmth of the sun. He did not push her away but made no move to embrace her.

'What if I've changed my mind?' she murmured.

He flinched. 'It's too late.'

'I wrote. You wrote back.'

'Yes. And I searched each one of your letters for a sign of affection or regret and found none. And then I gave up looking. You sounded lonely, so I replied.'

She gave an indrawn gasping sob: 'Oh God, I wish I knew how to love you.'

Then he did put his hand up to her shoulder. She could hear the smile in his voice. 'You do little for my self-esteem.'

They moved apart and continued their slow progress.

'Shall you stay on here much longer?' he asked.

'I don't belong here. There isn't anything for me to do. And it's such a small world, hidden away. But I'll have to see what happens about my mother.'

'Of course.'

'I hope you'll meet her.'

He laughed. 'I fear she would be too much for a simple soul like me.'

Before re-entering the house they solemnly shook hands.

'I do wish you every happiness, Sophia,' he said.

'Doesn't that sound straightforward?' she replied, smiling, but she scarcely knew how to release his hand, and could not bear to follow him inside.

Colin insisted on taking his evening meal at the inn. He said he wanted to leave the family together so at least Sophia was spared the embarrassment of confronting him and her father together. She was waiting for her father when he finally emerged from Harry's study, but was completely unprepared for the way he took her in his arms and embraced her. When she put her hands on his back she could feel his rigid spine through the soft cloth of his jacket. I cannot be forgiven this easily, she thought, or has anxiety for my mother at last softened him?

At dinner he was at his most genial and brought to the quiet Roundstones dining-table a polish and wit its conversation generally lacked. He listened with absorbed interest to Margaret's nervous chatter, asked Helen informed questions about her work and seemed quite able to discuss rural affairs with Harry though Sophia knew, from a remark he had once made, that he found the doctor's company tedious. Sophia said little and avoided his eye as she watched his charm work its familiar magic. Helen took off her spectacles and smoothed her hair, the most self-conscious gestures Sophia had seen her make, and Margaret, despite herself, glowed and giggled.

At first Sophia too was seduced by the excitement her father generated. All her life she had tried to win his goodwill – his approval, or more usually the absence of his disapproval had been enough to give direction to her day. If he kissed her, smiled, or said: 'What a becoming frock, Sophia,' she would retire to bed happy and wallow in the memory. Her weeks in Needlewick had allowed her to escape this distortion; she was able to live and evaluate and experience more freely though she could not of course completely shed his overbearing influence. But now that he was physically present again she found herself checking her reflection in the hall mirror, handling her cutlery more fastidiously and smoothing her voice for him. Her heart jolted when he smiled at her; when he asked her a question she stumbled over her reply.

But then she began to wonder what he was doing in this house where his wife lay sick in body and mind through years of struggle – years in which he had turned his back on her. When catching his eye Sophia recoiled, remembering that he had recently attempted to manipulate her future by his rigid outrage at her uncertain engagement, and she tried to arm herself against him.

Beyond an enquiry into Suzanna's well-being and a grave nod when Harry responded that she was still sleeping, he did not mention his wife again until after the meal. Neither man showed any desire to be left together so the entire family trooped into the drawing-room where Theobald remarked: 'A delicious dinner, Margaret. I'm sorry to have intruded on you this evening, but I felt so anxious about my wife. I can't leave you to bear the responsibility for both my wife and my daughter.'

'Oh they're no trouble at all! Dear Sophia has been such a help with poor Mrs Bubb. And I was so pleased to see Suzanna!'

'Harry suggests that it will be some time before she recovers and I cannot leave her here indefinitely.'

Sophia intervened with as much composure as she could muster: 'Mother must surely decide her own future, Father.' She felt that he was taking possession of Suzanna as if she were an old piece of furniture to be shunted about.

He smiled at her. 'Of course. If she is fit to decide for herself. Harry?'

'As I told your father earlier, Sophia, I have asked another doctor to call tomorrow – a colleague with some expertise in cases of nervous disorder. But she seems happy here for the time being.'

'I'll go up and see her now,' Simon Theobald said.

'No.' Harry spoke firmly. 'She must rest. She is asleep, and should not be woken.'

'I would like to look in on her, in any case.' Simon Theobald rose to his feet and Sophia realised that there was no stopping him, her uncle was no match for such strength of will. 'I'll come with you. If she's asleep we'll leave her,' she said, trembling with anxiety.

She led him up the stairs and opened the bedroom door. Inside, the room was dim, though the floral curtains were of thin cotton and outside there was still some light in the sky. Suzanna was curled on her side like a child, a plait of hair fallen across her face, but there was nothing childish in the way her fist was clenched on the pillow, the thumb caught under the fingers.

They stood at the door for a moment watching her, then Theobald went over to the window and drew back a curtain.

'We'll leave her,' Sophia whispered, 'as she's sleeping.'

But he beckoned her over to him. 'I wondered when you thought of coming home?'

'Probably with you, when you go.'

'I've missed you.'

'I'm sure the house has run smoothly without me.'

'It's not the same without you.'

'You seemed resigned enough to my marriage to Colin. I would have had to leave home then.'

'Yes. I wanted to apologise to you. I behaved badly. It was such a disappointment. I wanted to see my little girl happy.'

'I believe Colin will have told you that there is now no question of our marrying.'

'I was very sorry, but of course I understand.' His conciliatory words were so unexpected that she came near to taking his hand or even allowing tears to fall. Instead she said bravely: 'I thought I might enrol at college in London and work for some qualifications. I wondered about perhaps renting my own accommodation.'

Both knew she had no money of her own.

He asked, inevitably: 'What qualifications?'

'I'm not yet clear what is available. I thought of nursing or perhaps learning to type.'

This was a mistake. The predictable, obvious, yet contrasting nature of these two options betrayed the insubstantiality of her plans. Indeed, both suggestions had fallen off her tongue from nowhere; she had not thought of them before. But they were at Roundstones, in the twilight, and her father's apology still hung between them so Sophia felt that this was her only chance.

'Very well then. I suggest you come home and we'll make arrangements, perhaps for next year as I expect you're a little late to enrol for this autumn's courses.'

Sophia recognised that the first obstacle was being flung in her path. She raised her head and looked down to the river, a dull ribbon in the gloom. 'We'll see,' she replied.

When Sophia turned back to the dark room she could

see that her mother's eyes were open. She touched her father's hand and he went and sat by the bed. 'Suzanna, I came to see how you were.'

'I'm very well, thank you, Simon.'

He reached for her hand but she plucked at his fingers to tear them away. Instead he stroked her hair. 'My dear girl,' he whispered.

She began to weep. 'Make him go away, Sophia. Why is he here?'

'Suzanna,' he murmured, 'Suzanna, my dear love. Wouldn't you like to come home to me?' He clasped her hand in his and kissed it.

Suzanna, too weak to resist, gazed past him to Sophia. 'Please, Sophia!'

'Father, she's too distressed. Come away.' Sophia had never seen him display such emotion, yet she could not trust him. He was a man who could plan every word he spoke, every tear he shed. 'Father!'

She took his arm and led him out on to the landing, though she sensed his anger at not being allowed his own way.

Stupidly, in an attempt to comfort him, she said: 'Mother was telling me earlier about how you first met her near the Tunnel Woods.'

'God, the Tunnel Woods!' His hand was on the newel post as he turned to Sophia and his eyes were very blue and cold. 'I hope no-one told her I sold them a few weeks ago. She'd probably make a scene if she knew they are to be cut down and the land ploughed.'

*

Harry was waiting in the drawing-room. He seemed to have gained courage during their absence, because he spoke firmly: 'Perhaps you'd like to come back tomorrow afternoon? Then we'll have a clearer idea about Suzanna's condition.' He held Theobald's hat. 'I understand Colin – Lord Kilbride – is waiting to drive you back to Cheltenham.' He held the door open. 'Goodbye, Simon, until tomorrow afternoon then.'

Sophia stood on the stairs and watched her father adjust his hat. Then the door was closed behind him and Harry turned to her. 'You were right, I should not have telephoned him. He should not have come.'

22

Sophia could not sleep. Her mind teemed with memories of the day; faces, words, swam in and out of her mind and then she would come to herself and think wearily, Oh, I'm still not asleep then.

Small wonder I'm overwrought, she thought, my fate has been sealed today; I won't marry Colin, but instead go to college and become a typist. I will wear cheap shoes and a black skirt and take trams from one dirty area of London to another.

Her room in Roundstones offered no comfort because it was a harbour she must leave within twenty-four hours and a reminder that from it she had achieved nothing. Now she would never reach the clearing in the Tunnel Woods. Helen's diaries, stored in the bottom of her case, rebuked her. They had seemed to offer her the possibility of new direction, but all they had done was unleash unhappy demons from the past. And following her to Needlewick had come first her mother, then Colin and her father – all in their various ways to disturb the tranquillity of Roundstones. Everything that had happened had been blundering and unintentional. She had made several blind attempts to reach the clearing, released dangerous, festering emotion in Michael and perhaps even destroyed the fragile calm that Mr Gresham had restored to his life.

But at last she slept, dreamlessly and deeply, to be awoken at seven by an unusual bustle in the passage outside her room, cries and questions, hurried footsteps, Margaret's voice.

Sophia went to the door and called: 'What is it?'

Helen was standing at the top of the stairs in her nightgown.

'Your mother has disappeared.'

'I thought Uncle Harry had given her a drug to make her sleep.'

'It must have worn off.'

'She can't be far.'

'Sophia.' Helen took her by the arm. 'She had a photograph – I don't knew where she got it. There were two girls.'

'I know. I assumed Aunt Margaret had brought it down for her. Why is it special – two girls in a garden?'

'It's not the garden, it's the clearing in the Tunnel Woods.'

'But who are the girls? Who took the photograph?'

'The girls are probably our mothers. I can't tell for sure. And I don't know who took the photograph. Mother doesn't remember.'

Helen had lost her calm demeanour and was agitated, embarrassed by the drama of the situation. 'I think Suzanna must have gone there.'

'But she's so weak. It's so far. She can't have walked all that way!'

'I think she has. She will be there. So we must follow.'

*

A wicked wind had got up in the night and it must have rained towards dawn for the grass was very wet. Sophia was ill-equipped for an early morning walk against a robust autumnal wind – her wardrobe at Roundstones consisted only of light frocks, a couple of cardigans and a jacket. Helen walked doggedly, her head well down, dressed in a thick skirt and woollen jersey borrowed from her father. The river was muddy and fast moving, carrying no reflection, only its own silt. Leaves skipped along the path, whipped from the trees by this first wind of winter.

'What do your parents think?' Sophia asked breathlessly.

'They said it was worth a try looking in the Tunnel Woods. Father's gone to the village, in case she is there or at the Greshams or the church. Mother's mind is on the funeral.'

'But Mrs Bubb is dead,' Sophia cried. 'Surely she should be concerned for the living.'

'Yes, but what could Mother do anyway?' Helen seemed to understand her cousin's exasperation but made no attempt to soothe her. 'I hope Suzanna hasn't gone far. None of her clothes is missing, only her nightgown and an old bathrobe of Mother's.'

'What about shoes?'

'Her shoes were in the wardrobe.'

Although the wind knocked the strength from Sophia she was forced to do little running steps to keep up with Helen. Soon her legs were wet to the knee and her feet soaked. After a while she said to Helen: 'Thank you for taking the trouble.'

'I feel responsible. When I called in to see her last night she showed me that photograph and it took me by surprise. I said: "Good Lord, the clearing!" and she seemed terribly excited and said: "Yes, yes, I thought you'd recognise it."'

'But Helen, you're not to blame. It was Father who upset her by arriving so suddenly.'

'She told me that your father is going to cut down the Tunnel Woods. Was she right? I thought she was talking wildly.'

'Father spoke about it after we'd left her room last night. Perhaps he intended her to hear.'

'Could he be that cruel?' asked Helen.

Sophia didn't reply. She was so warm that the wind blowing on her neck was a relief, though strands of hair caught in her eyes and mouth. She took her cousin's arm. 'Helen, you do remember the Tunnel Woods, then? I thought you must have made yourself forget.'

'I hadn't forgotten. Not entirely.'

'What was there, Helen, tell me?'

Helen walked yet faster, her arm unyielding under Sophia's hand. 'Good Lord, nothing! A child's fancies.'

'But my mother was there, too. Why would she want to go back?'

'I don't know!'

'Helen, who was it really in the photograph? I couldn't make it out.'

'It was ridiculous of me but when I first saw that photograph yesterday I thought it was me in the clearing

– standing next to an unknown girl in a long dress, not you. But of course I was mistaken, how could it have been me? I was never there with anyone except you.' She stopped dead. 'I'm sure she's there. We should have brought other people to help bring her back. She'll be cold and exhausted. We should at least have brought a blanket or something.'

They hurried on, Sophia doubled up with a stitch, stumbling over rocks and roots in the path. The Tunnel Woods seemed to retreat.

By the time they reached the fence, rain was falling in cold shafts, soaking through their clothes and onto their backs and necks. Helen stood still at last, rain streaming down her face.

'Helen!' Sophia shouted. 'I know a way. This way.'

Helen did not move. 'Who built this fence?'

'My father probably. I know a way, along here.'

'Sophia, she won't have been able to get through. She won't have been able to find another way.'

'She might.' Sophia knew they must go to the clearing now so she plunged through the undergrowth until she found the break in the fence.

Among the trees the rain had as yet made little impact but soon great drops would begin to fall from the treacherous canopy of leaves. The woods were very still under the blowing tree-tops, as if tensed for the penetration of the rain. Now Helen led the way again, marching purposefully towards the tunnels, not faltering when a thorn caught at the back of her hand or rain dribbled from her hair into her eyes.

At the entrance to the tunnels she stretched out her hand to Sophia. 'Come on. Hurry.'

The tunnel was thick with stagnant darkness and the cold of the rain was nothing to the chill within. Sophia's only link with life was Helen's warm hand and the cuff of her wet jersey – she could smell the damp wool. But in minutes they were in the break between the two tunnels and Helen turned without hesitation to clamber up the steep rocky bank, though it was wet and slippery. At the top she helped Sophia before searching for the path through the bracken.

But of course there was no path. The bracken was now a dense forest reaching to their adult shoulders and higher, and the path Helen, as a child, had beaten with daily use had long since disappeared.

Panic and frustration welled up through Sophia's knees, thighs and stomach. 'Helen, you must remember the way.'

'Don't you see? There's no point even in trying. Your mother can't have come this way. The bracken would be trodden down.'

'She might be there. Wasn't there another path?' Sophia was shouting. They must get to the clearing. Helen must not give up now.

Helen plunged into the bracken, thrusting it aside with her hands, stamping with her feet. She did not pause to hold the heavy fronds aside and they slashed back in Sophia's face. Their legs were grazed by the sinewy stems. Soon they were submerged in rancid bracken, head-high as Sophia remembered it, but with no alluring little path to ease their way.

Then they reached the clearing. Suddenly the bracken began to thin and they were in an open space.

'She's not here,' Helen said at once.

Nothing was there but a small clearing in the woods, with a hawthorn tree in the middle, and grass flattened by the rain. The women were still, under the relentless rain.

'What will we do next?' said Sophia at last.

Helen was staring at the tree. 'You'll have to stay here. She might come after all. I'll go and look for her.'

'You'll get lost.'

'I won't. But you must wait here. This is where she'll try to come.'

'Shouldn't you be the one to stay?'

'I know the woods better then you.'

Helen seemed afraid, as was Sophia, of being left in this dripping heart of the wood. In a moment she had disappeared again into the trees.

So Sophia had reached her grail. But she had missed the enchantment before and could not find it now, because through her panicky adult eyes the clearing was small and unremarkable. The tree was perhaps rather larger than average and certainly very old, its leaves already tinged with the sad yellowing of autumn. It never used to rain here, Sophia thought angrily, looking to the sky for relief, but the clouds were thick and relentless.

She decided to shelter under the tree where it seemed a little drier; the leaves underfoot were not shiny with wet like the grass and when she picked up a handful they felt damp but warm. Crouching against the trunk, she drew her inadequate jacket about her. How foolish she had been to believe that her poor sick mother could have staggered all these miles.

The trunk against her back felt wonderfully solid compared to the pliable green stalks of the bracken, the flattened grasses, the steel shafts of rain. To be so still after the rush of activity made her feel faint and tired. So she closed her eye and listened to the rain on the leaves, the wind gusting over the tree.

A man would come with an axe; the weapon would gleam as the blade caught the sun, and he'd swing back his right arm and cut at the tree. And, after fifty or so blows, the tree would fall with a sighing compression of leaves and branches, and the heart of the clearing would be broken. Next he'd bring out his saw and hack at the branches until the tree was a neat pile of logs. Meanwhile the soft grass would be strewn with chippings and mounds of dead leaves hidden by the fallen tree.

Perhaps houses would be built here with neat gardens and pipes reaching into the soil which had nourished the tree, or a road would cover the earth and men's feet and men's machines would stamp on the hard stones.

And what of Helen's people? Were they waiting by the tree for Sophia to leave, ignorant of the disaster that was planned for them?

Sophia opened her eyes and stared into the pool of leaves.

Here was an end to her quest, waiting for her after all, singing to her as the wind in the leaves. I absolve you from dependency. I absolve you from being a victim of your mother's dreams or your father's ambition; from your passive, shared culpability for your brother's death and the unthinking destruction of your cousin's childhood. Knowing this, from now on, you are free.

She was alone in the clearing. The rain fell on the leaves.

'Sophia. We've found her. Sophia.'

In moving, she sacrificed her last fragments of warmth – the contact of her back with the tree, her drawn up thighs with her body. Helen was waiting on the edge of the clearing, wet hair straight as a helmet, clothes clinging to her stout body. They ran from the clearing, following the old path through the woods; the elusive, short-cut route which Helen seemed to have found without difficulty – it, at least, was not overgrown.

'Where is she?'

'Michael found her. She couldn't get into the woods, of course, because the path by the river was blocked. He made a shelter for her and now he's gone for help. She's in a terrible state, Sophia, she'd been trying to force her way through the fence.'

Suzanna was lying in a sheltered hollow near the path where bracken had been beaten down and where a dense undergrowth formed a rough tent for her. A man's jacket was spread round her shoulders and Helen's woollen jersey across her feet. Her hair lay in fair strands on the earth and her hands, arms, neck and face were scratched and bleeding.

Sophia knelt down and cradled her mother's head in her lap but Suzanna did not stir. 'That wicked fence,' Sophia cried. 'She would have been all right. She just wanted to go to the clearing. It was my father. He's always been in her way.' She held the cold body more closely. 'Mother, you'll get better. I'll look after you. I'll bring you back here and we'll find the clearing, we'll find what you were searching for. I'll look after you. I'll earn money and we'll work together.'

'They're coming,' Helen said.

They had brought blankets and a stretcher for Suzanna. They laid her gently down and covered her face. Sophia stumbled behind with Helen and they walked back along the top of the valley, leaving the Tunnel Woods, age old, nestling in the valley, impervious, vulnerable.

23

Two of us dead in one year, Deborah Parditer thought. How terrible it is to bury the friends who anchor us to life. Even Suzanna had been a constant. Even though at times she had been elusive and cruel, life was less safe without her.

It had been far easier to mourn Eleanor properly. Deborah had wept for her years of suffering and for the empty rooms and gardens at The Grey House where letters and callers had always been so welcome. On the other hand Suzanna, dead, stirred in Deborah the same mix of feelings as when alive, with the result that Deborah could feel little grief for Suzanna. Rather, she was relieved that her friend's restless, demanding spirit was at last at peace; that Deborah need no longer fear that word of Suzanna would suddenly come to disrupt her settled existence; that she need not worry Suzanna would turn up, dainty and elegant however ill-clothed, and make Eleanor feel clumsy and over-dressed. Even when very sick Suzanna had created discord in Deborah's staunch heart by returning late at night, too distraught to see her friends, leaving Deborah to fret and ask herself over and over again: How can she be too ill to see those who love her? It had taken all Deborah's considerable will-power to fight down the old feeling of resentful exclusion and make excuses to herself for Suzanna: She's very sick, she's very tired. Now, at last, that yearning to be loved by Suzanna could be laid to rest.

Surveying the company assembled in Needlewick churchyard, Deborah wondered how many shared this ambivalence towards Suzanna's memory. Certainly Simon Theobald, who stood straight and still, as he had throughout the service, and whose face betrayed no sign of emotion. The young man, Colin Kilbride, was somewhere in the church. A decent young man, self-effacing, how very kind to have stayed for the funeral, now he was not to marry Sophia after all.

Next to Deborah, Jane wept unashamedly and held George's arm for support. Jane's love for Suzanna had always been much more straightforward, Deborah thought, not far from complete admiration. She had regarded Suzanna as a being from another, unattainable world and therefore never attempted to emulate or equal her.

Margaret, by contrast, seemed very composed. Indeed, for one who had lost a faithful servant and a sister in the space of a week she looked positively jaunty. Good heavens, wasn't that a brand new hat? What a ridiculous cockade poked out of the brim – and surely her skirt was shorter than usual by at least an inch. Margaret seemed less anxious than for years, her brow was relaxed. What had done this? wondered Deborah. Was it because at last Margaret did not have to live in her sister's shadow? Deborah almost cried out at the sudden realisation that she had never seen Margaret without comparing her with Suzanna, even when Suzanna was far away. When she looked at Margaret she always thought: It would be so exciting if Suzanna were here or: Of course, Suzanna was the lovely one, Suzanna was the most gifted sister. Poor Margaret was never allowed to flourish. Only Harry, who now stood at his wife's elbow, had recognised her worth and for her sake tolerated the ripples Suzanna's great storms had inevitably sent flowing out even to Needlewick.

Unexpectedly, Harry raised his eyes and his gaze caught Deborah's. How much he understands, she thought. Dear Harry. But, as they moved from the graveside, it was John Gresham who sought her out and offered his arm. Poor John, who had just seen another fragment of his wife's life committed to the earth, yet who had enough self-forgetfulness to recognise Deborah's loneliness and come to her side.

At the churchyard gate, Deborah turned for one last look. Everyone had left except Sophia who throughout the ceremony had stood at a little distance from the rest of the family, face calm, hands firmly clasped together. Even as Deborah started towards Sophia, Helen went up and took her cousin's arm. Immediately Sophia put her hand to her eyes, as if her tears had been awaiting permission to fall.

As she and Helen at last walked slowly away, Sophia was struck by how the days between that wet morning when she and Helen had accompanied Suzanna home, and this day of Suzanna's burial in the loamy Needlewick soil, had passed as if she'd been in a sleep, disturbed by tormented dreams and brief awakenings. She remembered wishing that the slow march along the top of the valley, with one hand in Helen's and the other steadying her mother's bier, might never end. There had been a dogged purposefulness about that walk, a calm, a unity which she knew would be shattered the moment the front door of Roundstones was opened to admit them. And sure enough, time since then had been fragmented into sorrowful conversations, packing, preparing, weeping, with no truth, no reality to any of it.

Suzanna, even in death, had thrown Roundstones into disarray. Where should she lie? At last Harry's study was cleared and she was placed amidst the dark furniture and heavy medical volumes in the one room she must rarely have frequented. Sophia was intimidated as much by the room as by the body within and could not at first bear to visit her mother there. But she went once with Margaret to stand by the slight, white figure with its delicate hands.

'Do you think she was ever happy?' Sophia whispered.

'Why yes, Suzanna was always happy. At least, as a little girl, she usually got what she wanted.' They smiled at each other, ruefully. Then Margaret said: 'The trouble with Suzanna was that she could never forget herself. She had so many passions – she followed them all, sometimes ruthlessly, but she always kept a little bit of herself in reserve, could not give the most important part.'

'Why was that, do you think?'

'She never knew,' Margaret replied strangely. 'She was always trying to find something which would release that in her.'

'The clearing?'

'Oh yes, the clearing. There was perhaps an answer there.'

'What did she find? Aunt?'

Margaret made a small, impatient gesture with her hand. 'My dear girl, Suzanna always knew what she wanted from the Tunnel Woods. Everyone who goes there knows what they are looking for. And do find. Didn't you?'

'And you?'

'Oh I was like many younger sisters. I wanted only Suzanna's love. I was content with that.' She reached out and straightened a fold of her sister's gown. 'Do you know, Sophia, it is a terrible admission to make to you, of all people, but I feel happier for her today than I did on the day she married your father.'

Margaret went to a shelf and tucked a book into line with its neighbour, twitched a drooping white bloom in a vase on the mantel and moved to the door. 'Come along, Sophia, we've got so much to do. Susan Makepeace is still far too slow.'

In the evening, Sophia took a last walk to Needlewick. All along the lane she looked for Michael, so she could thank him for not bearing a grudge from daughter to mother. But there was no sign of him, and perhaps, she reflected harshly, she did not deserve the comfort that expressing her gratitude to him might have offered.

On the way up the High Street she passed the Makepeace cottage, and remembered her mother's words about the village still being poor. Is it poor? she thought, I hadn't noticed. She had never looked beyond the uneven fronts of the cottages and was too preoccupied to pay much attention to them now. Instead she found her mother's newly covered grave and stood for a while shivering under the grey sky and fierce wind that brushed through the old yew tree and blew faded petals and leaves from the rose bushes along the churchyard wall. The only sign of Suzanna was a rectangular strip of soil. Sophia laid her hand on the cool, crumbly earth. I wish I could at least be sure that I loved you, she thought.

Then she moved on towards The Grey House. Afterwards she thought that Mr Gresham must have been expecting her; when he showed her to the drawing-room she saw that a fire had been lit and glasses and a decanter set out on a table by the window.

'Thank you for coming to the funeral,' she said. 'We all appreciated it. It can't have been easy, another funeral.'

'How are you now, Sophia?' he asked.

'I'm all right, I suppose, perhaps a little lost. Everyone's leaving tonight or tomorrow. Actually, Mr Gresham, that's one of the reasons I came to see you. I'm hiding from all the bustle. I hope you don't mind. Everyone's going off with a fixed purpose, except me.'

He led her to a chair, poured her a glass of sherry and they sat together at the window watching the weakest leaves from the apple tree skate across the grass.

'I'm to drive home with Father and Colin in the morning,' she continued at last. 'I expect you've heard that Colin and I definitely won't marry.'

'Do you mind?'

'I feel bruised, of course, but only, I suspect, because in the end it was he who decided, not me.'

'What will you do instead, Sophia?'

'I think now I will go to Zurich after all, to see the people my mother was with, and then I suppose I must find a means of earning my keep, since I have no wish to be dependent on my father.'

'How is your father?'

'I never really know. Disappointed, I suspect, more than anything. We've all let him down in our different ways.'

The room, when she fell silent, was so quiet that the tick of the little china clock on the mantelpiece sounded intrusive. Sophia's heart was beating fast, she was afraid she would not have time after all to complete her mission. To give herself courage she looked at Mr Gresham and found that his gaze, as always full of tenderness, was fully on her, not, as was more usual, a little averted as if fearful of actual engagement.

'Actually I also came to thank you,' she said at last, 'for everything you've done for me. You've been so kind. I didn't know you before this summer, I didn't remember what you were like, I suppose I was too young. And I wanted you to know, because it seems so sad and point-less that you shouldn't, that I love you for that, and for everything else. I didn't realise until now what it meant to feel like this about someone, just warm, and glad to be with them. And soft. Oh don't worry, I don't mean anything else by it, or expect anything.'

She had not stopped to question, when planning this visit, what his reaction would be. He sat very still in his chair, then laughed suddenly, replaced his glass on the tray at his side, held out his hand to her and led her out of the french windows and along the stone path to the gate. There he took her in his arms and rested his cheek on her hair.

'You are a precious girl, Sophia,' he said. 'You have brought me so much light.'

Half an hour later, Deborah Parditer called, as promised, to discuss the funeral and to suggest that he take a holiday. He was waiting for her at the garden door and surprised her by taking both her hands and kissing her on both cheeks. 'I've laid out the glasses,' he told her. 'I'm sure you'll be wanting a sherry.'

'A sherry would be very welcome.'

When their glasses were filled they toasted the memory of Suzanna Callwood. 'And Eleanor,' said John.

'Of course, Eleanor.'

'And life,' he added, 'which I find, after all, is full of rather delightful surprises.'

Sophia took the field path to Roundstones, the memory of John Gresham's embrace lending a lightness to her step. The sky was overcast; in a strong gust of wind a fine drizzle fell. The ground floor of Middlecote Hall was already lit, as was Roundstones across the valley.

At the footbridge she performed one last rite; she removed the diary from her pocket and held it over the rail. It cost her no pang to drop it into the fast-flowing, opaque water. The exercise books floated along bravely;

with little patches of darker red appearing on the thin covers, they sailed out of sight.

'There we are, Mrs Gresham,' she said. 'I've let them go. And I believe you'd say now that what I do next is entirely up to me.'

A WAY
THROUGH
THE WOODS

Reading Group Notes

In Brief

John Gresham looked at the two photographs on the small table. The young man in the uniform must be the lost brother, he thought, the slight girl he hardly recognised, Sophia. His attention was brought back to the room by Sophia's arrival.

Sophia wasn't aware of his wife's death and was genuinely upset. When he told her of his wife's bequest her upset turned to confusion. Mrs Gresham had left a couple of notebooks to Sophia which had once belonged to her cousin Helen. It seemed that Helen herself would rather the old notebooks had been destroyed, but had given them to Mrs Gresham as she'd asked for them. Helen certainly didn't want them now. The other odd thing about the bequest was that Sophia would have to go to Needlewick to collect them. Sophia couldn't see how she'd have the time – her wedding was scheduled for September and there was so much to be done.

As she dressed for dinner later that day she reflected. She was getting ready too early, almost deliberately stretching out the oppressive hours ahead with her fiancé Colin and her father. She remembered the visit she had made to Needlewick – she'd been fourteen and her brother had the measles. To remove her from the risk of infection she'd been sent to stay with her Aunt Margaret in Needlewick. How strange that summer had been.

Her mother ought to be told of the death of Mrs Gresham; she was her dearest friend. But goodness knows where her mother was now, and she never wrote.

Although Sophia couldn't spare the time for a trip to Needlewick her father was very keen on form, and a pre-nuptial visit to her relatives was the proper thing to do. Perhaps she should visit and collect her bequest at the same time. Needlewick was where her mother had been born, and it wasn't so far away, was it? Somehow, though, she didn't want Colin there, but she decided that she would go.

As Sophia travelled towards Needlewick on the train she remembered her fourteen-year-old-self on her previous trip. Had she really taken so many dresses? Still, her cousin Helen had appreciated them. It had been tiring, leading up to this pre-wedding visit, with the pressure of her father's irritation weighing her down. She didn't understand why he seemed cross about her trip, as he was so keen on doing things correctly. She supposed Needlewick had different associations for him; but still . . .

Sophia's aunt and uncle met her at Cheltenham in

a motor car. As a country doctor her uncle certainly benefited from the modern transport, and as he had to make a house call in Needlewick, Sophia and her aunt happily walked up to their house, Roundstones.

Sophia was disappointed that Needlewick didn't match the watercolour image she'd kept in her mind for so many years. It was rather an unremarkable little village, but as they approached Roundstones Sophia's disappointment with everything was suddenly chased away: Roundstones was even prettier than she remembered – and what a view over the valley.

After a greeting from the housekeeper, Mrs Bubb, that demonstrated that Sophia still wasn't liked, she entered Roundstones. Sophia had been happy here, she realised, until the tears at the end. And she'd not been happy since. She felt somehow distanced from life now, when it had been so immediate here at Roundstones.

But what had her cousin Helen thought of her visit all those years ago? Well, she'd find out soon enough when she collected the notebooks . . .

ABOUT THE AUTHOR

Katharine McMahon was born in north-west London, and studied English and Drama at Bristol University. She is the author of seven novels, including the Richard & Judy Book Club selected *The Rose of Sebastopol*. She has worked as a Royal Literary Fund fellow teaching writing skills at the Universities of Hertfordshire and Warwick. Katharine lives with her family in Hertfordshire.

THE STORY BEHIND
A WAY THROUGH THE WOODS

Katharine McMahon, 2009

Like *Footsteps*, this book began with a photograph, or rather a set of photographs, in this case the famous pictures of what are known as The Cottingley Fairies. The photos were taken in 1917 by two cousins – the oldest of whom lived in the village of Cottingley in West Yorkshire – who claimed that the fairies were real. The elder cousin, Elsie, was 16, the younger, Frances, 10. One of the reasons the photos were taken seriously by the public was that Arthur Conan Doyle, celebrated as the creator of Sherlock Holmes, and a Theosophist (devoted to the theory of a spiritual hierarchy) believed that they were authentic.

What intrigued me about the photos was not whether or not they were of real fairies (to my mind they were clearly fakes), but the temerity of the two cousins who claimed, right up until the 1980s, that at least one of the photos was a true picture of fairies. The date the photos were taken, in the middle of a war that was anything but fairy-tale, also struck me as significant.

So I decided to write a novel in which one of the girls is a dreamy, lonely country child, Helen, inhabitant of the village of Needlewick, whose life in 1912 is turned upside down by the arrival of her sophisticated London cousin, Sophia, forced to spend a summer in the country because her beloved brother is suffering from measles. Sophia is rather full of herself and thinks she's doing her cousin good by descending upon sleepy Needlewick in her London frocks and with her London ideas about sex and relationships. However, in 1920, after the war in which she loses her brother, and her family is broken up, Sophia is confronted again by the events of the 1912 summer and finds herself painted in a less than idyllic light.

It seemed to me, as I wrote the book, that those Cottingley fairy pictures were an odd relic of a world in which catastrophic violence and slaughter was happening on a scale never before experienced. As a result, the book is about the trauma of awakening from the sleep of myth to the harsh reality of the world. My book, in so many ways, turned out to be about the journey from innocence to experience. A reader of the novel is not required to believe in fairies, only that the Tunnel Woods, and what goes on in them, are in some ways a symbol of initiation. Girls who enter the tunnels come out changed. They learn about sex and betrayal there. They are confronted with their own true selves, and with the temptations of adulthood.

But what the book also became, as I wrote it, was an examination of what it meant to be a woman in the early twentieth century. When Sophia returns to Needlewick in 1920 women have just been awarded the vote. Her feckless mother, who has chased romantic illusion all her life, has moved on from the suffragette movement and is packing food parcels in Switzerland, so Sophia is left all by herself to face a future filled with conflict and difficult choices. Because in the end she rejects both her father's preferred world, in which the woman agrees to married submission, and her cousin Helen's decision to cut herself off from relationships altogether and bury herself in work, Sophia's future is wide open.

So a novel which began with the premise, 'How did those two young girl cousins dare to claim they'd taken photos of fairies?' ended up, in a gentle way, to be all about daring. But it is also about tearing the paper-thin veneer on that Edwardian summer of 1912, when nothing was quite as it seemed. Mrs Gresham, the astute looker-on, is dying; Michael, the outcast, is actually the one who knows most about everything; Sophia's sophisticated home-life is falling apart, and Sophia, who believes herself to be blessed, is actually far worse off than her plain country cousin, who is so firmly rooted in the community of family and friends.

But perhaps the last word (but one) should go to the fairies. Like many children, the boundaries between the real and the imagined world were blurred when I was young. In researching fairy mythology, I found it intimately connected with nature, the seasons, chance, superstition and folk lore. For Helen, in the novel, the world of fairies is as real as all the other things she doesn't understand. It is unpredictable, exciting, just out of reach, and a powerful link between the present and the past.

To some extent, *A Way Through the Woods* now seems to me to form part of a trilogy with *Footsteps* and *Confinement*, novels which explore womanhood at a time of monumental change – suffrage, war, machines, the gradual erosion of the class structure. As such, it's quite a serious novel, though with a light touch; under the preoccupation with frocks and fairies are much darker questions. Its original title was: *Beneath the Leaves . . .*

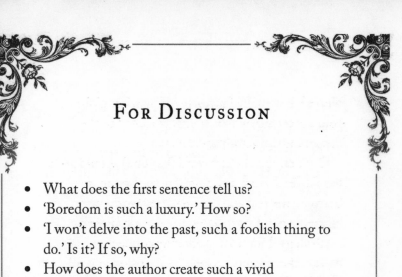

FOR DISCUSSION

- What does the first sentence tell us?
- 'Boredom is such a luxury.' How so?
- 'I won't delve into the past, such a foolish thing to do.' Is it? If so, why?
- How does the author create such a vivid atmosphere?
- 'Sophia says she does not like sitting under trees because you never know what might fall on your head.' What does this tell us of Sophia?
- 'She can't understand the meaning of anything you can't touch or buy.' Is this a fair assessment of Sophia do you think?
- 'You should never be afraid to leap alone.' Good advice?
- 'Sleep came easily in Needlewick.' Why?
- 'It's always a mistake to be too dependent on one person.' Is it?
- Why does Sophia know it's time to leave Needlewick when she sees the garden at The Grey House?
- How does the novel examine the contrast between the small world of Needlwick and the wider world?

- 'It was my father. He's always been in her way.' How was he in Suzanna's way?
- 'The trouble with Suzanna was that she could never forget herself.' Is Sophia at all like Suzanna?
- How has the changing role of women affected life in Needlewick?

SUGGESTED
FURTHER READING

Atonement by Ian McEwan

The Case of the Cottingley Fairies by Joe Cooper

The Portrait of a Lady by Henry James

The Go-Between by L P Hartley

The Forgotten Garden by Kate Morton